NORT__
SOUTHWEST

An Anthology
by
North Bristol Writers

Margaret Carruthers

Roz Clarke

Clare Dornan

Desiree Fischer

John Hawkes-Reed

Kevlin Henney

Jemma Milburn

Ian Millsted

Justin Newland

Pete Sutton

⬤ Tangent Books

North by Southwest
Edited by Joanne Hall
First Edition Published in the UK
by Tangent Books
with the assistance of the BristolCon Foundation

Tangent Books, Unit 5.16 Paintworks, Bristol BS4 3EH
0117 972 0645

This edition © Tangent Books; Miss Butler and the Industrial Automaton Group © John Hawkes-Reed; A Bristol Pound © Jemma Milburn; Lye Close © Ian Millsted; Christmas Steps © Pete Sutton; Gardening Leave © Clare Dornan; Fisher of Men © Justin Newland; Top of the Hill © Clare Dornan; A Halloween Tale © Margaret Carruthers; House Blood © Ian Millsted; Latitude © Pete Sutton; Uncle Lucas © Clare Dornan; Hater © Pete Sutton; Taxi Driver © Desiree Fischer; Noon Train © Roz Clarke; Like Giants © Kevlin Henney

ISBN: 978-1-910089-11-8

Cover illustration and design © C M Hutt
Interior illustrations © C M Hutt

www.tangentbooks.co.uk
www.bristolcon.org

A CIP record of this book is available at the British Library.

Printed using paper from a sustainable source.

ACKNOWLEDGEMENTS

This book would not have been possible without the tremendous support of the following people and companies:

Joanne Hall and Claire M Hutt went above and beyond the call of duty and deserve special praise.

Joanne Hall for stepping in as editor and for her professionalism
Claire Hutt for her inspirational artwork and irrepressible good humour

We are also extremely grateful to:

Jemma Milburn for creating the North Bristol Writers Group
Richard Jones for all his support and advice
Tangent Books for facilitating the publishing process
BristolCon for their support above and beyond our expectations
Fundsurfer for providing a platform to raise the funds
Oliver Mochizuki and Derek Ahmedzai for all their support during the funding efforts

Additional and heartfelt thanks are due to Jonathan L Howard

The following people pledged money to our Fundsurfer all of whom have our lifelong thanks and appreciation.

Julian Hicks, Sarah Dattani, Ian Millsted, Amy Morse, Sammy H K Smith, David Gullen, Philip Purser-Hallard, Andrew Goodman, Arthur David Smith, Richard Sewell, Lindsey Turner, Gavin Watkins, Mike Manson, Ade Couper, Karl Hughes, June Burrough, Huw Powell, Jonathan Clay, Dan Pawley, Alistair Rennie, Kevlin Henney, Claire Fisher, Pete Sutton, T. L. Anderson, Sue Beale, Cheryl Morgan, Joanne Hall, Kathryn Jeffs, Bernadette Lewis, Matt & Emily Turnington, Sarah Ellender, Stephen Bryant, Derek Ahmedzai, Roz Clarke, Richard Jones, Claire M Hutt, Carol Ward, Denise Denson, Eddie Winthorpe, Desiree Fischer, Hoz Shafiei, Alan Stidwell, David Redd, Louise Gethin, Jari Moate, Tom Abba, Tim Dornan, Nicholas Carter, Clare Dornan, Jo Lindsay Walton, Sarah Ash, June Burrough, Rosie Wabe, Tom Greer, Mary Christmas, Andy Bigwood, Green Lane Films, Bernadette Lewis, Oli Morgan, Darren Morrissey, Andrew Robertson, Lhizz Browne, Tom Hartney, KatJeffs, Andy Dingley, Ben Holder, Dan Pawley, Jodi Quinn, Richard Bendall, GiantkillerRich, Emily Turner, Luke Wiles, Jon Clay, Samuel Mansfield and Eliza Ross

CONTENTS

INTRODUCTION

I was invited to write the introduction to this book just before I went on holiday. To my delight and – dare I say relief – I discovered that *North By Southwest* actually makes perfect holiday reading. Each story is self-contained and there is such a wide variety of styles and flavours contained within that I found myself picking up the book (at that point a messy pile of A4 print outs), curious as to what the next piece would hold. I read some of the stories without looking at the authors, trying to guess who was behind them. To my surprise, none of my guesses were correct! Either I never considered the style of these particular comrades thoroughly enough, or they have enjoyed themselves by being wholly creative and varied.

Indeed, the variety found within these pages is bound to entertain. There are short pieces to fill a stray half hour, and longer entries to really sink your teeth into. There's a lot to get you thinking, and a few that will send a shiver down your spine!

Kevlin's LIKE GIANTS is a display of primordial and soulful poetic rhythm to get those literary cogs turning. From the normality of a loving family bond Clare achieves something simultaneously charming and chilling in UNCLE LUCAS – whatever the age of a character, they have a perspective from which a story can be told, Clare develops a voice that can evoke loyalty, or, in THE TOP OF THE HILL, sheer terror. This darkness is also apparent in GARDENING LEAVE, one of the longer stories in the collection.

I just want to take the time to sit down and rehearse Desiree's THE TAXI DRIVER aloud. Here is a man you need to listen to. He's old, and his wisdom could change your life

If you want to escape into a longer adventure, then John provides us with anthology opener MISS BUTLER AND THE INDUSTRIAL AUTOMATION GROUP, a thoroughly entertaining exploration of character and mechanical marvels. While Roz's NOON TRAIN is a suspenseful ride to the end of the line. This is a short thriller which makes you care passionately for the characters and their cause.

Pete spices things up with some creepy undertones, in LATITUDE, a true adventure ending in... well, I can't tell you. While CHRISTMAS STEPS paints you into a beautiful scene that can only end in tragedy. I secretly enjoyed reading HATER, perhaps for the delight of indulging in another person's twisted gratification. Like exploring another person's house, I followed this strange character through his day, peeping through the keyhole into his brutal mind. I just hope it isn't based on anybody real!

Ian takes on a strange future Bristol with an undercurrent of savage beauty in HOUSE BLOOD, and there are more haunted houses in Margaret's A HALLOWEEN TALE.

Keep reading... There is still more adventure to be had!

Join Justin's protagonist on a voyage from Bristow's harbours to a new land, accompanied by an infamous FISHER OF MEN. In a style perfectly suited to the subject, the story offers a vivid sense of a faraway place and time.

If you want to know anymore... you need to start reading the book!

The support the writers have given each other has really become apparent in the editing of the submissions. *North By Southwest* has been a team effort to be proud of.

North By Southwest has been beautifully illustrated. Claire Hutt has provided artwork inspired by the contents of these pages, a project in its own right.

North Bristol Writers was born the moment the phrase "Let's just do it, why not?" was uttered in response to a problem. The problem being that there wasn't an open and inclusive creative writing group for people who simply want to write as a hobby in our neck of the woods. The original idea focussed on writing activities that brought budding novices together. As with any young club, commitment is key and establishing numbers to make it stable takes time. I am glad we have put the idea and the name of North Bristol Writers out there. This was a foundation which said "Hey, we exist and want to do something!" It was just waiting for one person – Pete Sutton – to stumble into it and decide to do some building!

The firm establishment of North Bristol Writers was down to the dedication of its members through the early stages. People were determined enough to get involved in a group that was only just maturing. The release of this anthology has given us further focus and heralds the development of North Bristol Writers into a well-established and productive group. Many of the participants are active on the local literature scene, running their own groups and events, or writing and editing for publication. It is an honour to have them on-board. North Bristol Writers exists to provide a fun and safe environment for people who enjoy being creative. There is no level of experience required to be involved but I hope that within these pages you will find a showcase of the variety that can be achieved through collaboration.

By Jemma Milburn
Founder, North Bristol Writers Group

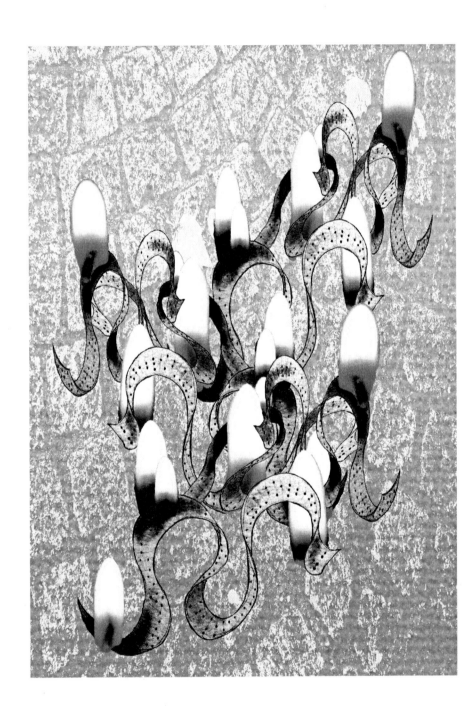

MISS BUTLER AND THE INDUSTRIAL AUTOMATION GROUP

by JHR

It was the day the test elephant exploded.

I was already hiding behind the big stable door with Hoskyns when the screaming from its turbine changed from a noise I could hear to a pressure somewhere behind my eyes. I'd never heard one do that before, and I crouched low with my hands over my ears, willing someone or something to arrive and put the poor beast out of its misery.

There was a dull slapping noise and everything around me jumped. The top half of the door bounced away down the yard, spitting big splinters as it tumbled end over end. I was enveloped in a cloud of steam and dust and hauled a handkerchief from my sleeve for something to cough into. When I could breathe properly again, I scrubbed my eyes and discovered Hoskyns looming over me and miming something. All I could hear was the final whine of the turbine, so I pointed at one ear and shrugged. He scowled and held up a finger. Be a good girl and stay out of the way while the men deal with the dangerous thing. I scowled right back and scrambled to my feet – Hoskyns had been my driver cum tutor cum minder for a year and a half and should know damn fine who was going to be most use at poring over the entrails of a detonated steam elephant.

When I peered inside what had once been a stable block,

I scowled again at the state of the test stand. I was going to get wrinkles, look prematurely aged and who-knew-what-else. At least that was what the voice in my head was telling me. I ignored it, gathered my skirts in one hand and began trying to work out which pile of smoking remains was exploded elephant and which was demolished test stand.

From the door, the elephant looked like it had slumped down in the far corner for forty winks. Only closer inspection, when the dust cleared, revealed that the dark patch on the lower flank wasn't a shadow but a human-sized hole punched through the steel plate by most of the high-pressure turbine impellers. Judging by the white scar in the black brick floor, that was where the rapidly-moving shrapnel had ricocheted before ripping away the top half of the stable door on its journey into the next county.

I edged round the pool of hydraulic fluid – I rather liked this pair of boots – and leaned over to peer up into the body cavity. Shards of turbine casing had bounced around enough to make a proper mess of the inside.

"Is it safe, miss?" Hoskyns had clambered over some remains and was eyeing the hydraulic pool from the other side.

I shrugged. *Not your fault* I reminded myself. *It wasn't screaming in pain – it was a mechanical contrivance going badly wrong, and the best thing you can do is find out why.* I was terrible at taking my own advice.

"Someone will have to rescue the card-book from the Jacquard when the casings stop being red-hot," I said. There was almost no tremble in my voice at all.

#

Steam Elephants don't explode. Or rather, the War Department had made it very clear that randomly killing the crew would be bad for morale. Thus the steam and hydraulic systems had safety valves that were set by a man at the factory. When they went pop, as frequently happened, the crew piled out and brewed up while waiting for the Engineers to arrive. Meanwhile, the Jacquard wouldn't even run until the turbine was up to speed.

I stopped dead in my tracks and inspected the outer edge of the card-book. All the bindings looked new, but since the thing had suffered a light steaming, it was hard to tell if anyone had tampered with the code by pasting in a duff card. I stared up at the back of the Theosophical Society building, wondering how to explain my suspicions to the Colonel. There was going to be a board of enquiry and the most likely explanation was going to be some unforeseen mechanical failure because of substandard castings or mice in the grunge wheels. And that *was* the most likely explanation. The Colonel and Zoe and Hoskyns were going to shake their heads patiently and call me a silly girl for even suggesting someone would be able to make an Elephant explode, and even more preposterous was the notion that they would be able to do it by sneaking *something* into the Jacquard commands. I turned the card-book over in my hands. I knew what the original code should look like because I had written most of it myself. However, this was a newer book, and because the Colonel had been keeping me busy, I would have to go and ask someone what some parts did. That would be frustrating and embarrassing and lead to the sort of questions to which I only had angry answers. Ugh. No, I was going to work this one out for myself, no matter how long it took.

I was on my third circuit of the grand central staircase when I had one of my better ideas. The late afternoon sun was streaming through the big rose window, lighting up the greater part of three stories of stairwell. I scampered up the last two flights and looked about me. Aha! There it was. A brass shell-casing that served as an ashtray for people who liked to lean on the banister and stare out at the gardens behind the Theosophical Society. I opened the card-book and tipped the end out into space, hoping it didn't rip itself to pieces as it cascaded open. I weighed the cover of the book down with the shell-casing and beetled back down to the floor below to survey what I had wrought.

The entire Elephant program hung down over two-and-a-half stories. I sat on the landing carpet, leaned forward to rest my head on the stair-rods and tried not to concentrate on any particular part of the book at once.

Code has patterns if you look at it in the right way. In the same way that the sounds of a train journey are a set of repeating patterns, or the noises made by a properly running Elephant are more pleasant than one that's been maintained by someone with no manual and a big hammer, so the code that controls that running has patterns of its own that can look 'right' or 'wrong'.

I didn't spot it straight away. I could see the original walking code, and my patches that allowed the Elephants to run without destroying their knee clutches. It wasn't until the sun reappeared from behind a cloud that two extra runs of holes revealed themselves on the far left-hand edge of a handful of cards more or less level with Colonel Elliot's face. He had braced his hands against the fourth floor banister and was peering out into the stairwell to see the bottom end of the code-book. He looked back up and raised his eyebrows when he saw me watching him.

"Miss Butler," he said. "I'm sure you have a most entertaining explanation for this." He gestured at the gently rippling column of cards.

"I do. Sabotage."

#

Eighteen months ago, I was a mostly-useless youngest daughter. Then I proved I was a better Jacquard-hacker than, oh, everyone at my father's factory, which led to something of an adventure with dock-cranes animated by the captured spirits of the recently dead. This meant that I was a sad disappointment as a youngest daughter, but the Colonel and his group of Jacquardistes, ex-soldiers and otherwise adventuresome types fell upon me like the returning prodigal. Or maybe I was the fatted calf. Some days it was hard to tell.

Thus I spent several months under the tutelage of Miss Zoe Harker, in which we discovered how little we knew about each other's fields, and what felt like far too long with Sergeant James Hoskyns, in which we discovered I could probably hit a barn with a 20-bore shotgun, assuming I was inside with the doors closed.

#

"Now then," said the Colonel. "Sabotage? How? And why?"

I sat back in the chair nearest the window and rifled through the code-book until I found the unidentified slots. "This is probably the how," I said, brandishing the book at the Colonel.

He peered at it over his half-moon spectacles.

"I think we'd better send for Miss Harker, don't you?" He scribbled a note, folded it into one of several small cylinders scattered on his desk and stuffed the message-capsule into the Lamson tube bolted to the side of the fireplace. There was a muffled thump as the vacuum dragged the capsule towards Zoe's office which was next to the big Jacquard in the basement.

There was another thump, followed by a chime as a new capsule bounced off the 'You have a new message' bell. The Colonel inspected the contents and peered over his spectacles again.

"Miss Harker commands me to tell you, and I quote, 'Do try to keep the silly girl from killing herself until I can arrange for tea and cake.' So."

I started to protest, but the Colonel held up a finger like a cricket umpire giving 'out'.

"I have already sent Hoskyns off to the bosom of his family so he can recover. I'm sure you'd prefer I didn't afford you the same opportunity. So, again, tell me about your trip to Malvern."

"I pitched up at the Royal Steam Research Establishment as instructed, and spent the morning being wheeled about the boring bits by some old sweat who ran on pink gin. When he nodded off after his second lunchtime brandy, I toddled back off to the works under Malvern Wells that he'd carefully avoided."

The Colonel was nodding and scratching notes. I carried on.

"There was a huge square-and-compass above the entrance to the tunnels, which rather gave the game away, but there was something terribly odd about the square – my eyes seemed to slide off it, and if I tried to concentrate on the thing, I started to see a kaleidoscope and the left hand side of my head began to ache. It was a lot like the square wasn't actually square at all. I pressed on into the main hall, where there were a dozen huge steam locomotives in various states of repair, attended by chaps dressed in heavy smocks and goggled helmets. It reminded me of Piranesi and Breughel all at once."

"Did you find it?" said the Colonel.

"I did. Whatever they're using for fuel in those engines, it's not coal. Coal does not glow blue. I scooped a trowelful into that blasted lead-lined handbag you had me cart around like it weighed nothing and scarpered in the general direction of Malvern station and points south-west." I paused. "Do you know what it is yet?"

The Colonel wiggled a folder from under several message

canisters and tapped it. "Not really. Rutherford's being a donkey about it and insists the stuff comes from West Africa. I think you're on to something with the Masons, but I don't think the ritual they follow is one that would be familiar to anyone on this earth."

I folded my arms. "Martians? Spirits? I know we're in Madame Blavatsky's back bedroom, but *really*."

The Colonel sighed. "You should keep an open mind, Miss Butler, especially given the circumstances of our first meeting. No, not spirits nor Martians. I think that mineral comes from a place where geometry doesn't work and our laws of nature don't apply."

"I think you're going to have to explain that," I said.

"You're familiar with the hollow earth theory?"

I considered rolling my eyes at this point, but as the Colonel pointed out, I had shot a distress rocket into the control-cabin of a marauding dock-crane from a howdah atop a steam elephant.

"Holes in the poles?" I said. "Yes, Charles Fort is quite illuminating on the subject."" Between Jacquard-hacking and failing to shoot anything, I had been able to lose myself in the library for days at a time. Getting to the section marked 'esoterica' had involved scaling 'particle theosophy' and an interesting traverse through 'computational philosophy'.

"Very good. There are many stories of entrances to the 'inner earth' being scattered across the surface of the globe, one of which was apparently discovered by a Staffordshire ploughman in the 18th century. It would not surprise me to learn that those locomotive-filled tunnels under the Malvern hills go somewhere very strange indeed."

"And this entrance is guarded by something that looks like a Masonic lodge, but is in fact something else?"

"Oh, I think *they* think it's all normal enough, but their particular

Great Architect is far stranger than they realise – most people wouldn't have paid proper attention to the square-that-isn't-square."

There was a cough and a rattle of saucers from behind me.

"Debrief complete?" said Zoe, from the far side of a tray of tea and cake.

"I think so," said the Colonel. "That is, unless Miss Butler has anything to add..?"

I held up a finger. "Debrief?"

Zoe handed me what looked like a tureen of tea and a quarter of a fruit cake. "You've heard of a briefing, yes?"

I nodded and wondered where to put my prizes. There was a clatter as the Colonel swept some more message-canisters into a wicker bin. I leaned forward to perch both cake and tureen on the edge of his desk.

"Well, then. Briefing and debriefing. We've sucked your brain clean of all the terrible things..."

I raised an eyebrow. I very firmly doubted *that* statement.

"... And now we can talk about something else," said Zoe, settling in the wing-back chair opposite mine.

I paused to gulp tea. I seemed to have been doing rather more talking than I expected. That was odd.

"Such as?" I said.

Zoe grinned. "Such as these extra slots you've found in the Elephant code-book."

"We have three mysteries, I believe," said the Colonel. "First, what are those extra slots; second, who put them there; and third, why?"

"Four. Four mysteries. *How* did someone get that code-book into the test elephant?" I said.

#

The day after, I was careful to wear the boots and day-dress I had found most suitable for scaling the library shelves. The sensible thing would have been to go and inspect a Jacquard-7, but the only one close at hand was now scrap, since it had taken a direct hit from a flying turbine blade. Father would have had one or two in a half-completed elephant, but there'd been an 'incident' at the works and there would be no more Jacquard-7s for the foreseeable future.

The smaller Jacquards had been built originally by the crypto-masons at the RSRE, so if you wanted to know anything about their internals you had to petition the War Department, who would huff on about 'national security' and tell you nothing.

That was the official version, anyway. The sort of people who seemed best suited to hacking away on Jacquards were also the sort of people who'd generally have alarm clocks and/or frogs to bits as children to see how they worked. Tip-top Jacquard hackers were generally the ones who'd been able to put the things they'd disassembled back together without any parts left over and without leaving a trail of clockwork frogs or leaping clocks.

They also liked to share their discoveries with like-minded souls, which was why I was descending with a box-file containing the complete run of '2/6d – The Jacquard-Hacker Quarterly' clutched one-handed to my bosom. Next time I'd borrow a newsboy's bag and leave both hands free for not falling to my doom. Or at least the risk of a turned ankle and a lecture about proper decorum in the library. Honestly, if they're going to fill a room with full-height shelves and hide all the interesting books in the top two rows, what on earth do they expect?

Half an hour later I skidded to a halt in Zoe's office and waved a copy of 2/6d at her. "Found it!" I squeaked.

She held up her hand and continued methodically stabbing holes into a card-book. I knew that state, so I stood there and tried not to bounce up and down. I could interrupt her, but she'd lose the logic sequence in her head and while she'd be gracious about it, it would take her another twenty minutes to get back to where she'd been and when I've been in that same position I have cheerfully contemplated bloody murder of the interrupter.

"What have you found?" she said after a while.

I brandished the magazine. "This!"

Zoe sat back and scanned the article. About halfway through, she began nodding, then looked up and grinned at me. "By Jove, I think you've got it. We should report this upstairs."

#

"A steam-organ?" said the Colonel.

"Yes." I was pacing between book-stacks while Zoe egged me on from the sidelines. "Some careless sort drove a showman's wagon into a Steam Elephant outside Tenbury Wells, and in the confusion before a policeman arrived, a couple of enterprising fellows had a good look at both the Jacquard in the Elephant and the remains of the wagon, which had been a Wurlitzer-164 dance organ. The card-reading mechanisms were startlingly similar, according to the reports. Which is all very well, but as the saying goes 'code-book or it didn't happen'. So I took the opportunity to beetle down to the music shop at the top of Christmas Steps and discovered this."

I hauled an organ-book out of its brown paper bag and dropped it on the Colonel's desk. He peered at it, then turned to dig the suspect Elephant code-book from wherever he'd hidden it. He laid the books side by side and flipped through the cards. The programming was obviously different, but the layout of the cards was distressingly similar. He stopped flipping the code-book when he came to the section with the mystery slots, but continued working through the organ-book until he found the same format slots.

"Excellent work, Miss Butler," he said. "What do you suggest as a next move?"

I looked at Zoe for moral support. She made a shooing motion. I guessed that meant she was happy for me to take charge.

"I think I would like to find out what 'IAG, Oxford' might be, because that's where the original report came from."

The Colonel nodded. "Very well. That seems as good a lead as any. Miss Harker, could you warm up your Jacquard to see what intelligence we may already have? It might be best to keep that job under your hat and run it overnight."

Zoe stood. "As you wish." She turned to me. "Olivia, could you go back to the music shop and enquire about those slots in the cards?"

"I could. But do you think it might be a bit obvious, going to the nearest shop to the Theosophical Society and starting to ask about the inner workings of steam organs?"

"Good point. Do we know if there's an organ works in the area?"

"Tewkesbury," I said without thinking.

Zoe and the Colonel goggled at me. I felt myself blushing the way I did when I'd called one aunt or another an idiot one Christmas.

"I had to change trains in Worcester last month. There was an advertising hoarding. It had a surplus apostrophe, and that stuck in my head because I wanted to find a brush and paint it out..." If I'd been a phonograph my voice would have deepened as I ground to a halt.

#

"Miss Butler? I trust you had a pleasant trip." Mr. Blacker appeared at the door of his organ works as I hove into view. He peered round on the off-chance a male guardian or minder would arrive and make everything better.

I pasted on a smile and inclined my head. "Thank you Mr. Blacker. I did. I hope the Colonel's telegram provided enough of an explanation?"

Blacker nodded vigorously. "Yes indeed. Do you have anything specific you would care to view?"

"I think it best if you lead me through the workings of a dance organ from card-book to vox humana," I said, watching with glee as Blacker's train of thought lurched across an unexpected set of points. The time I had spent on the train speed-reading an organ manual had achieved the desired effect.

He collected himself and pointed the way into the depths of his workshop. "Very well, Miss. We'll begin with this Galvioli that's had rats nibbling at the trumpet motors."

#

The inside of the organ works, like the insides of the works of organs, were an awful lot more interesting than I had imagined. Once Blacker recovered from the fact that I was female and started treating me like a willing apprentice with a strange line in overalls, his passion for the work was a joyful thing to behold.

"So you see, when they stopped needing to pay a lad to crank the organs by hand and could run them from a steam engine, they ran into a different problem. You see, a boy will stop work when the organ-book finishes, but an engine will just keep going. When there's no more book, all the valves open at once and it sounds like the Second Coming. So what they did was add an extra control-line right on the edge of the register, out of the way of the musical scales, that worked backwards. When that valve opens, everything else is shut off, and since no organ books are cut there, it makes no odds to the old organs. When the book comes to the end, there's not a racket to startle the horses." Blacker had a different component on a workbench and was pointing out the holes at the far end, set slightly apart from the rest.

I was trying very hard not to seize the thing off the bench and run all the way back to Tewkesbury station, cackling all the while. It looked exactly like the read-head from the Jacquard-7, as described in the 2/6d reports.

"Is that a Wurlitzer-164 part?" I said.

Blacker blinked and smiled. "Yes. Yes, it is. This is the famous one, as it happens."

"Famous?"

Blacker snorted. "Bristol's not too concerned with goings-on out in the sticks, eh? Enough of your own news, is it? Well, can't say I'm surprised. You know it was the Mop Fair last month, at least?"

I did. I nodded and smiled agreeably.

"Good, good. So. This organ here," he said, tapping his fingers on the thing, "is the property of Tonks' Travelling Fair. Mr Tonks has a prime pitch right up by the railway entrance. It also turned out to be ideal for some toffs to hitch the thing up to a traction engine and pinch it. Funny business, mind. The police found them in a barn round the back of Northway. They'd set up a limelight, had the organ to bits on the floor and were photographing all the parts."

Blacker shook his head to indicate the impenetrable nature of the ruling classes. I joined in because I had a nasty idea that this was all connected with the correspondence in '2/6d' and I didn't much care for where it might be going.

"Caught red-handed, then?" I said.

"Yes. And up before the Assizes at Gloucester the next week. They were set to go straight to gaol when some fellow, name of Smith I think, gets up on his hind legs and begs the magistrates forgiveness and could they see their way clear to letting them off with a fine. Says they're just students and they let the excitement of discovery run away with them or somesuch, no harm done, generous donation to the showman's benevolent fund and would everyone mind just looking the other way?"

Blacker had stopped tapping the woodwork and now had a rather firm grip on a mallet. He seemed to realise what he was doing, relaxed his grip and breathed out.

"Students?" I said.

"So they said. 'Industrial Automation Group', I think they called themselves. Anarchists, more like."

#

I charged into Zoe's office at the crack of lunch the day after. "What do we know about the Industrial Automation Group? I think they're part of an Oxford college..."

Zoe flapped one of her outsize Jacquard cards under my nose.

"IAG. Based at the Clarendon building and something to do with Keble College. Although it seems that they're considered a rum bunch by some of the dons. They *were* just seen as a harmless lot of far-too-forward thinkers who'd been left to play with cogwheels as children." She paused.

"But?" I said.

"You remember the fuss at the National Physical Laboratory the other month?"

I nodded. "Mob of impostors posing as Canadians, wasn't it? Wandered into one of the Jacquard test-cells and installed a bogus card-book. Which is why we don't have a Jacquard-7 to play with. That was IAG?"

Zoe poked another of her cards in my direction. I wished I could read it. Code was my thing, and this was, well, code as well, but not Jacquard-7. I wanted to stomp off and hide and have dark thoughts about never being clever enough because the mechanical control stuff was so easy and this was just a different Jacquard so that must be easy too and the only sensible explanation was that I was too dim to understand Zoe's stuff and that just made me want to scream.

"Hoi. Breathe, will you?" said Zoe.

I blinked repeatedly and took several calming breaths as instructed.

"Yes. IAG. And…" she waited until I met her gaze. "What was all that about?"

I could have made some excuse, but I just glared at her. "My mind is going. I can feel it."

"Pish. What's really going on?"

I'd have flung myself into a chair and propped my feet on something, but all the chairs were piled with books from the library or card-books from the Jacquard. Instead I paced and counted things on my fingers. "It seems to me the trouble started with that wagon-crash up near Tenbury. Someone got a look at both sets of works, put two and two together and made six. But, I mean, that's just interesting. So what if the works of the Jacquard-7 are made of clockwork mice? If it makes the thing better at, oh, I don't know, making tin elephants trot about the place, then that's a good thing. Anyway, the next thing we know is someone's managed to pinch a fairground organ of the exact same type, just so they can pull it to pieces and photograph the works. They're also arrogant enough to send in a tame beak for special pleading and to wave some cash at the problem to make it go away. Then they walk into the NPL in broad daylight and detonate a test Jacquard, which again feels like some rotten oik has booted over your sandcastle for no other reason than he can. Finally, they managed to blow up *our* elephant while Hoskyns and I were standing there, which is really quite far from cricket. That means they've infiltrated some hateful code into our standard steam elephant library, and until we find out where that code-book came from, I'm not sure I'd trust any steam elephant not to explode where it stood. Bad enough that it makes us look like a complete shower of idiots, but imagine what would have happened if it had been a parade or something? The carnage doesn't bear the thought. We'll have to work backwards though the versions in the code-library to find the last known good one and then work out what the differences are. I guess if we hang the things over the banisters again, that'll make life easier. And if we start with a code-book that's about halfway through the age range, that would cut down the number we'd need to look at by at least half."

"Your brain's going, is it?" said Zoe.

I shrugged. "That's all basic stuff. Not like your cards there. I can't even read them. It's like being rubbish at French again and being expected to recite Molière in front of people. I still have nightmares about that."

Zoe pointed one corner of her card at me. "This isn't even English. It's John Wilkes' analytical language, which is still officially a mad idea which does not work, either because you can't possibly construct a workable ontology via human language or because a given religion expressly forbids it. However, if you start with Enochian, it becomes a trivial matter of coding. The hard part is decomposing machine-generated Wilkes grammar emitted by an Enochian compiler into English. As you have discovered."

\#

The porters at the station eyed the woman travelling alone and without much luggage with appropriate suspicion. I tried to look like the sort of person who wasn't considering diving under the wheels of a train, and they let me wander off to the far southern end of the platform, well past the last of the fire-buckets and the flower bed with the name 'Kingham' picked out in pansies and whitewashed stones.

My station allowed me to take notes on the disposition of the 'special excursion' laid on by Keble College as it huffed to a standstill. A carriage filled with 'horseplay' and 'good sport', two wagons with cable drum frames containing large discs under green tarpaulins, three flatbeds with steam elephant-shaped lumps under more green tarp, two goods vans, a further carriage for the working types and a long GWR guard's van that I hopped on to when everyone else was looking the other way.

Hoskyns peered over his paper at me and nodded to the chair on the other side of the Tortoise stove. "Afternoon, miss. There'll be tea and buns when we're moving. Pleasant journey?"

I growled at him and flung myself into the chair.

"Yes, miss. I quite understand that posing as a member of the lower orders for a few hours is a remarkable imposition. Why, I was saying as much to Mrs. Hoskyns the other day, and we were both amazed that we'd borne up so well under the strain of it all, and for so many years."

I sat up so I could see him over the kettle that was starting to sing to itself. "That's not it at all. It's just that... I thought it was a much better idea to go along to the Clarendon Building and see what they were up to."

"That's as may be, but since we still don't know how they managed to get their own code-book into our elephant, we have to assume they know more than us. And that means you can't pitch up on their doorstep without questions being asked. Chief among those questions would be 'What's a girl doing expecting to come in here?' I'll be bound. This way you've a perfect excuse to wander among the suspects and fill them with alcohol, without it being anything other than business as usual."

I scowled for form's sake, but the awful thing about the entire enterprise was that I knew damn fine it was our best chance to stop being a step behind. The other awful thing was that Hoskyns was entirely correct, too. I slid back down in my chair so he couldn't see my mortification.

Two stations later, Hoskyns folded his paper and wedged it into a small cupboard with the rest of the kindling. "Right, miss. I believe the show starts at the next station. I'll nip forward and brief the locals while you get into character."

I let my unbuttoned coat slide off my shoulders and onto the chair to reveal the black uniform I'd been wearing all morning, then stepped forward to execute a mildly wobbly curtsey. "As you say, mister 'oskyns."

He tutted, rolled his eyes and shook his head. "I think it might be as well to turn the wick down a little. More Mayfield Park and less sound-of-Bow-Bells."

#

The train pulled into a siding at Mickleton station. We were transported in charabancs through a nearby village to a stately pile of a manor. I watched as the students were herded inside the big house and was casting about for an excuse to follow them in when I was hauled away by one of the housekeepers and set to work helping lay out an enormous cold lunch at one end of the marquee pitched on the lawn. Once in a while I could see Hoskyns steaming past with an armful of wine bottles, but I was unable to do anything but get on with the task I'd been handed. Some time later, the students trooped back out again. I couldn't pay too much attention, but some of them looked a little green around the gills. I was soon delegated to the head wine-waiter and told to make myself useful with a couple of bottles of red.

There were three different groups of students – the handful who'd looked entirely uncomfortable on leaving the manor house and who were the sort of people my father would have called 'bedwetters', a much larger group who seemed to be having a whale of a time helping themselves to their host's wine-cellar, and a final collection of six or eight who were setting about the cold buffet with single-minded efficiency. They were drinking as much as the larger mob, who would shortly fall to bread roll lobbing and party games involving trousers and fire, but it was as if they were from a different train and were making the best of an unfortunate double-booking by studied Englishness and ignoring the revelry around them. One or two of them glanced up as I made my rounds with the wine, as if put out by the intrusion into their personal bubble, but otherwise I was soundly ignored. As best as I could tell, the 'Cahill rotors' were performing satisfactorily, the differential guidance apparatus would be fitted by the time they reached the starting line and the 'girl guides' were still flapping about like headless chickens.

I tried to work out what on earth they were talking about as I returned with fresh bottles. I was no further forward by the time I reached the quiet end of the tent, so I made sure to take my time refilling their glasses and wondered how I might goad them into revealing more information. The fellow who I took to be in charge of the group turned to his companions as I worked my way round the end of the table and said, "Of course that buffoon Elliot will get nowhere hiding behind the skirts of his tame suffragettes..."

I narrowly avoided pouring the rest of the wine up his sleeve, and I was firmly tempted to empty the other bottle over the arrogant little oik's head, but I maintained control as best I could and made to vanish in the direction of the rowdy end of the table so as to report to Hoskyns. Instead a hand closed firmly round my wrist and the same voice said, "Got you."

#

I was dragged into the manor house, propelled up a grand staircase and escorted only mildly roughly into a vast bed-chamber. My captor pushed me onto the bed, then took up station by the door. I made to bound off the bed and fly at him, but he pulled a small pistol from his pocket and said, "Sit. Stay. Good girl."

I seethed and did my best to melt the gun with the power of my glare alone. On one hand, I seemed to have flushed out the core of the group. On the other hand, I'd failed at spying and everyone would have to pretend not to be disappointed. Assuming I emerged from this particular fix with a dressing-down instead of a eulogy.

"I must admit I was interested to discover what sort of female would have the guts to take so much credit for men's work, but it seems you're just another English idiot who thinks they can wrap honest men around their fingers. And that disguise, well..." He barked a laugh and pulled out his pocket-watch.

I leaned forward to plant my feet against the floor, hoping to rush him, but the aged four-poster creaked as I tried it.

"Don't." My companion didn't even look up.

I settled back on the bed, accompanied by further creaking, and tried a different tack.

"I fear you have the advantage over me, Mr..."

He allowed himself a brief smile. "I do, don't I? Smith, for the purposes of this conversation."

"You can't shoot me," I said, wishing it to be true. "They'll hear you downstairs."

"Ha. The inbred aristo scum are too busy drinking, and the

scholarship boys will do what they're told lest they get found out and laughed back below stairs where they think they belong. No-one will rush to your aid, Miss Butler. Anyway, enough talk. There's water and a water closet through there. The windows might open, but I don't suppose the creeper will bear your weight. We'll be back in a few days when we'll put either you or your corpse on a train back to Bristol. Try not to make a mess." He backed through the door and made sure to lock it as deliberately as possible.

I waited until I heard him trotting down the stairs before making a bee-line for the door and tugging hard. It didn't budge. Not even a rattle. A swift tour of my accommodations revealed some bookshelves filled with gothic novels, a bathroom and WC as advertised and windows ditto. Since this room overlooked the greenhouses and formal gardens at the back of the house, waving and banging on the windows was going to get me nothing but a sore hand.

I flung myself onto the bed and sulked.

#

I finished feeling sorry for myself quickly enough – Hoskyns would be along soon and I would just have to put up with whatever he, Zoe and Colonel Elliot threw at me. I toured the room again, prodding at odd panels in the hope of finding at least a priest-hole, if not a secret passage. Since that failed to produce anything useful, I worked one of the windows back and forth against the forces of paint and rust. Although there was a handy down-pipe, the creeper really wasn't up to much and the flower beds did seem an awfully long way away.

I stopped for a moment to listen. The noise of drinking and cold lunch seemed muted, as if they were drawing further away the longer I remained a prisoner. Lunch. There was an apple and a scotch egg next to the Bradshaw in my bag, which was under the bench seat at the back of the charabanc. I was going to be ravenous by the time Hoskyns arrived to effect rescue. I yawned, crawled to the centre of the four-poster and lay back to stare at the canopy. It took me a moment to recall where I'd seen the scenes in the tapestry. It seemed it contained all the illustrations from the alchemical text 'Splendor Solis' – there was the knight on the double fountain, the miners cutting into the hill and, directly over my head, the sun rising over the city. It felt like a terribly odd thing to keep in a bedroom, and I wished I could explore the place, rather than having to charge off after the IAG. I yawned again. I could hear people-noises over the sound of pigeons, larks and a distant cuckoo. I wished the people would shut up so I could listen to the lark properly.

#

The sun was at the wrong angle. I bounded off the bed and stuck my head as far out of the window as I dared. More larks, a distant pheasant and a low-pitched whistle from the railway line. It was as if the excursion had never been here. I was going to have to rescue myself. It would be me, a length of cast down-pipe and questionable brackets that may or may not have been inspected in my lifetime. I tried very hard not to think about what I was doing as I crouched on the windowsill, facing the locked bed-chamber door. What was the most complicated library-climbing? Was it rescuing the Lions Book from the top shelf above the door after father had one of the footmen take the ladder away? I had one toe on a bracket, wedged firmly between down-pipe and wall. I gave it an experimental wiggle. Nothing felt like it was moving, which probably meant I hadn't wiggled hard enough. Or, if I wiggled harder, it would part company from the house and swing out sideways with me clutching the top like a rope trick gone wrong. I grabbed a handful of creeper.

There was a crunchy tearing as the less able suckers gave way.

What about the other week when Zoe was watching? That involved a traverse through Particle Theosophy and then swinging through the doorway at head-height into the non-human languages section. I had been completely showing off that time because Zoe was there. I took hold of a fresh lump of creeper, which ripped away from the wall without ceremony and dumped me into one of the ornamental Box bushes planted either side of the drain-cover in the flowerbed.

I whirled around to make sure that no-one had seen my somewhat daring escape, but it was still just me and the local wildlife. I had rescued myself.

I stepped out of the flowerbed, crunched across a gravel path and onto the croquet lawn. There were ornamental beds to the left and right, but ahead was door set into the high wall that surrounded this part of the gardens. I needed to get back to the front of the house, and forward seemed to be the way forward. I made for the door and hauled it open with a fan-shaped scrape of moss and gravel.

Everything was slightly wrong.

I was in a sculpture garden. I could see the stone pineapples that marked the roof of one of the greenhouses over the dense privet hedge to my left. At far edge of the space was a low balustrade broken by what looked like a stairway to a lower terrace. When I turned to look back through the doorway, I found the door itself shut and over-run with ivy, and the hinges and latch rusted solid with age. I thought about scaling the wall, but the door was set too deeply into the wall for me to be able to swing myself over the top. If I wanted to go back, I'd need to find a ladder.

I made my way towards the nearest sculpture. It was the sort of mask I'd last seen on a member of a Greek chorus, but easily twice my height. As I neared the thing, I realised that rather than facing me, I was on the inside and it looked outwards across the terraces of the garden. There was a set of white marble steps and ship's porthole where the pupil of one eye would have been, the former obviously an invitation to peer through the latter and survey what lay beyond.

I peered. The brass of the porthole framed a second sculpture, although it was less sculpture and more architectural sample. It was an Italianate staircase that rose from a cluster of ornamental shrubs and curled up and around to stop abruptly where it met its supporting wall end-on. It was hard to make out details because it was bleached white by a mid-day glare. As I watched, a woman in a servant's uniform similar to mine approached the base of the stairs. She paused, one hand on the balustrade and staring at the space where the staircase would go, when something disturbed her. She turned and hurried off in the direction of the greenhouses. I clattered back down my own staircase and charged round to the front of the mask sculpture, but she had vanished.

I made my way to the second sculpture. As I walked past the shrubs, I felt someone was watching me from behind. I stopped at the base of the stairs – something about this seemed very wrong, but my train of thought was interrupted by a muffled yelp from the direction of the greenhouses. The woman in the dark outfit. I steamed off towards the noise, rounding the scrubby end of the privet hedge to find myself in the gardener's yard. There was no sign of the woman. A greenhouse took up most of the facing wall. A long open-fronted shed was at ninety degrees to that, facing the hedge. In the centre of the yard was a large incinerator, the contents of which were smouldering quietly. I peered into the thing to discover it half full of partially-burned paper. I tried to haul out a good handful, but the edge of the incinerator was jolly hot. I squeaked, flapped my burned hand and went to search the shed for a pair of gloves or a fork.

I didn't fancy the idea of carrying a pile of carbonised documents, so I forked the lot into the nearest wheelbarrow and set off with it to find my way back around to the front of the house. Instead, I found the entrance to the kitchens was unlocked, so I hauled the barrow past the kitchen range and up the back stairs into the entrance hall. The long room on my left contained a suitably large table, so I parked the barrow and started to work through my charred burden.

There seemed to be three sorts of document, or parts of document. Engineering drawings, some of which made references to the 'Cahill Rotors' and some which seemed dreadfully familiar; maps, which were mostly too burned to be useful; and what seemed to be anarchist tracts or pamphlets containing more capitals and exclamations than entirely healthy.

The tracts appeared to describe an imminent scourge which would befall right-thinking men unless action was taken. Things had gone too far and our modern age was awash with the terrible results of allowing some second-rate types far too much leeway in running things for their own benefit. This was illustrated by a smudged bulldog in a union-flag waistcoat being held at bay by a mob of women waving Suffragette banners. Further engravings showed an Elephant in mid-explosion and a man carrying an injured child. Their intent was clear, and I backed carefully in the direction of the map-fragments. It was like trying to put together a jigsaw that had been in a nasty accident. I tried to find all the corners and edges to begin with, but I soon discovered I had at least three different maps. One of a city, one of fairly lumpy countryside, if the density of contours was any guide, and one that was beyond hope. I slumped in a chair, rested my chin on my arms and eyed the countryside map. Something about the lay of what hills I could make out was bothering me. It was as if I'd been there before.

I growled in frustration and stalked round the table for another look at the engineering drawings. Whatever-it-was seemed to be packed into a person-sized space and had a pair of connectors about yea-far apart on one side. I held my hands out in front of me to get a better idea of what yea-far looked like. Left-hand one just described an arc fore and aft, while the right-hand rig rotated. I pushed through the charred stack. There had been another half-burned paper that looked something like a dome or cupola. Aha! I'd bashed my head on the inside of that dome-shape so often I'd stopped thinking about it. It was a cutaway view of a steam elephant pilot's position. Two sets of Marconi equipment were mounted on the spaced armour each side of the pilot, which was replaced with a mechanism that obviously connected directly to the elephant's control gear. Why? I straightened and tried to stretch the kinks out of my brain by staring at the ceiling. When I rolled my chin back down, the first thing I saw was the collected parts of the countryside map. From this angle it was obvious why it seemed familiar. I'd spent a happy summer wandering that area of Scotland as a small child.

I stretched again, yawned, and cast about for a clock. There were bookcases and paintings lining the dark panelled walls, but nothing else, and the light had changed again. The gloom deepened as I watched. I held my breath and listened for the measured ticking of a long-cased clock. Nothing. Even the wildlife had packed up and gone home. I wanted to search the grounds for the charabanc with my bag and I wanted to find Hoskyns and I wanted to find a post office so I could send a telegram to the Colonel informing him I was on my way to the Scottish lowlands and mostly I wanted to lie down for a nice long nap. I folded up the two most interesting parts of engineering drawing, looked around for somewhere to put them, remembered that my bag was somewhere else, cursed the lack of storage in my current dress and then stomped off up the big staircase to see if I could find a way back into 'my' room from the inside.

#

Leadhills station hadn't changed much. The last time I'd been there, I was about the same size as the steamer trunk that I accompanied to the grand house my older sister Mary had married into. This time the porters weren't fussing over the 'wee lassie' visiting the big house so much as looking down their noses at the dishevelled serving wench who was obviously no better than she ought to be. I spent the first part of the walk to St. Johnston House composing a long sequence of remarks and conversations in which I cut them all dead. However, the sun was out and there were sheep, larks and spectacular hills, and I was able to lose myself in the glory of it all.

The house sits in a notch of land halfway up a low hill. The stream running down the back of the notch has been diverted to run a hydroelectric plant for the lights and the collection of workshops surrounding the stable yard. This means the main approach is a switchback drive through tiers of enclosures that start as rough pasture and become more and more tilled the nearer they are to the house. There is usually someone doing something to some plant or livestock. Today there wasn't. It was rather eerie. More eerie was the way in which the front door was flung open as I was about to belabour the knocker.

"You."

"Yes," I said.

Mary glared at me. "Didn't father marry you off to some curate to avoid this sort of nonsense?"

I blinked. It was true there'd been a gleam in father's eye when Elmstone Hardwick pitched up disguised as a curate, but the entire pretext was to find me, rather than father. He was also a captain and at the time was the Colonel's right-hand man. The Colonel hadn't recruited anyone new in the eighteen months I'd been there. Was I now his right-hand woman? I suppressed a smirk.

"*Captain* Hardwick lost his life in the course of his duty," I said. I was itching to say 'helping me shoot rockets into possessed dockcranes.' But of course that was a total secret and Mary would assume I was fibbing.

She shook her head, then dropped the lady of the manor act and smiled like the big sister I'd hoped for.

"Oh, come here, you little idiot. Everyone's been worried sick."

I saw Hoskyns slide into view as I peered over Mary's shoulder while she hugged the life out of me. I waggled my eyebrows in greeting and he nodded.

We trooped into the back kitchen. I looked about to see where the housemaids and cooks were hiding.

"I sent them all back to the village for safety," said Mary when I asked. "Would you like tea?"

I looked at Hoskyns. What was he doing here anyway?

"It's been nearly a week, miss. Where have you been?"

"Tea. Yes. And a bath and... How d'you mean 'nearly a week?' The chap in charge at that bunfight dragged me off at pistol-point and locked me up like a princess in a tower. I duly loitered while waiting to be rescued by big strong men, who singularly failed to arrive. So I rescued myself, found the secret plans, hopped on the next train and here I am the very next afternoon."

Mary pushed a blue-and-white striped mug in my direction. "Tea," she said.

Hoskyns rubbed his face, as if trying to sharpen his chin to a point. He turned to Mary. "Do you still have that box the Ministry sent, ma'am?"

Mary raised an eyebrow. "Yes, I do. It'll be in the workshop next to the lighting plant, on top of the ammunition cupboard. And don't you ma'am me, James Hoskyns. Not now."

Hoskyns pushed himself upright. "Right you are, ma.. Mary." He turned to me. "I searched the manor and its outbuildings as soon as that party were back on the train. The place hadn't been inhabited for some time. Please be so good as to give Mary a full account of your movements. I shall be back shortly."

"Is this a debrief?" I asked.

"Yes indeed, miss."

I gave Mary a full account that began with Gloucester station and a bad mood. Hoskyns had returned with a suitcase by the time I'd got to the pistol-waving parts, and proceeded to assemble some sort of apparatus while I walked them both through the sculpture garden and the smouldering documents. I was able to haul the sheaf of documents from my bag and spread the remains of the maps and drawings along the table. I pointed at the contours of the hills. "That's the route from Leadhills. That's when I knew to come here."

Mary and Hoskyns exchanged a look. I'd seen that sort of thing before, usually just before Zoe or the Colonel explained something complicated and secret. She shrugged. Hoskyns looked pained. I got the impression he'd just been volunteered to explain what was going on.

"Miss Harker's Jacquard provided information to the effect that our friends at the IAG had offloaded part of their cargo some miles south of here, and had continued on north of Glasgow with the remainder. Since your elder sister has been part of the team for a number of years..."

I started to ask about fifteen questions at once, but Mary squeezed my hand and treated me to the big sister raised eyebrows that meant 'Just wait a moment, please?' which I suddenly remembered I missed quite badly.

"... I took the first train here. There is a formation of Steam Elephants moving in a straight line towards Glasgow. They will be here in an hour, when we will stop them. Now, would you be so kind as to look into this apparatus?"

I started to ask about Mary, then thought better of it and started to ask how we would be expected to stop a squad of Steam Elephants when all ours were out of action. Hoskyns was holding a couple of Bakelite knobs and looking expectant and impatient at the same time, so I leaned forward and peered into the eyepieces he'd indicated. It seemed to be a stereoscopic view of the Dutch House on Bristol's high street, but at the far end of a kaleidoscope.

"Try to concentrate on the view at the end," said Hoskyns.

I concentrated on the sign that read 'Tilly', which made me wonder if they were the same Tilly that operated the crumpet factory in Cheltenham.

"Thank you, miss. Did you by any chance see something like this?" Hoskyns pushed a photograph across the table.

It looked like a guts of a generator set connected to a small turbine. There were what looked like magnets surrounding an armature, as expected, but the armature windings defied inspection. I just couldn't focus on some parts of the photograph. I tried, but it felt like I was trying to hold myself cross-eyed, which seemed terribly familiar.

"Are those things that look like magnets actually the same glowing stuff I lifted from underneath the Malverns?"

Hoskyns looked slightly uncomfortable. Mary did her best not to look too pleased.

"Was I that good when you were training me?" she asked.

Hoskyns took a deep breath. "It would be wrong of me to comment," he said. "Nevertheless. Yes, you were." He turned to me and tapped the photo. "That is the field generator from a Temporal Dynamics Mk2 heavy displacement unit, and yes, it does indeed use the same sort of mineral you so helpfully collected the other month. The one in the picture is missing its shields, which is very bad news for anyone in the general area should someone spark it up."

"Bad news how?" I echoed. I was starting to worry about the direction of the conversation.

"In the worst cases, the operators are the ones displaced instead of the cargo. That rarely ends well. If lucky, everyone goes home with a world-class migraine and only wishes they were dead. In the middle, limited exposure will mean your subjective experience of time can become somewhat non-standard for a while. Longer term exposure..." Hoskyns shrugged. "It's not something we've tested."

Mary had a death-grip on my hand again.

"My... What? Time? Is that why you think I've been gone a week?" Part of me was wishing for the Theosophical Society library so I could read up on Charles Fort's views on 'non-standard experiences of time.'

Mary had plastered on a fixed smile. It was not an encouraging sight. I glared at Hoskyns instead.

"Yes," he said. "Days may have been shorter or longer for you. You may also have experienced echoes of your own actions."

"How long was I exposed? I mean, that is where this is going, isn't it?"

"A couple of hours. It was in one of the bedrooms." The two crisp snaps of Hoskyns closing the suitcase echoed in the kitchen. The coal in the cream enamelled range crackled to itself. Further away there were outdoor noises – pigeons, swifts darting out from under the eaves of the buildings in the yard, the dull roar of the forced-draught furnace in a Steam Elephant overlaid with the whines of steam turbines and hydraulic pumps.

"That's an Elephant." It was a statement. I didn't want to know about exposure to whatever-it-was. It was too large a problem to think about without it hurting. Fixing Steam Elephants was something I could manage. "What about the code-book? Is it safe?"

"It's still running your 1.0 version," said Mary. "The post up here can be a bit spotty, so we didn't get the most recent volume right away. And, um, Gerald left it on the hall table with some circulars, which proved a little too tempting for one of the Labradors." She shrugged and made a face. "A jolly lucky escape, really."

"1.0? But that's simply years out of date. Surely the cards are going round the edges by now. Why are you still using it?"

Mary favoured me with another big-sister look. "Because, you silly girl, I am very proud of what you achieved with it. You made the Elephants work when no-one else could, and you showed up Father, which added to the joy."

I blushed furiously and glugged tea to cover my embarrassment. I was always going to be the baby sister who was either pushed around like a toy dog in a pram or ignored completely when there were balls or point-to-point to think about, but once in a while I felt like a grown-up. I coughed the tea back into the mug. This was not one of those times.

Hoskyns waited until I recovered my composure. "Regarding Elephants, I think we should probably go hunting." He stood, and patted his jacket pockets as if looking for a pipe or keys. He pulled a cigarette case from an inside pocket and handed it to me.

"Keep this with you at all times. If you happen into the gentleman with the pistol again, toss it to him," he said.

I inspected the thing. It seemed to be made of Whitby Jet and bound in silver. The front was featureless save an indent marked with a square, while on the back there was what looked like a stylised view of an apple with a bite taken out. There were a couple of buttons set into its side, presumably the mechanism to open it. I made to press them both to see how the cigarettes were arranged inside, but Mary laid a warning hand on mine.

"Don't," she said. "Not here."

I raised an eyebrow, but did as I was told and stuffed it into the depths of my bag.

#

"What on earth have you done to the poor beast?" I had my hands on my hips and was staring up at the superstructure of the Steam Elephant in the stable yard. There was a sketchy turret behind the armoured dome of the driver's position, more or less where a mahout would have been on a flesh and blood example. Behind that, where the howdah should have been, was a monstrosity. It was obviously a turret, but there were pairs of medium-sized cannon mounted on either side. I pointed at the funnel-shaped muzzles. "Those. What are those?"

"Quick-firing two pounder autocannon, miss. Loaded with a combination of armour-piercing, tracer and high explosive rounds. If you'll follow me..."

We clambered aboard. The sketchy turret turned out to be a birds-nest of hydraulics and actuators with a reclined metal seat in the centre that seemed better suited to a mad dentist's lair.

"Driver or gunner, miss?" said Hoskyns.

"Gunner," I said. I wanted a closer look at the mechanism. I gathered my skirts in one hand and hopped down into the centre of the works. I shuffled round and looked back up at Hoskyns.

"The control is on the right arm. You'll need to pull the safety pin from the trigger, but please don't do that until you really need to."

I settled back and tucked my skirts behind my knees. There was a suspiciously small pistol-grip sticking out of the right-hand armrest. Any shovel-handed squaddie would have the devil's own time with it, but it fitted my own hand unsurprisingly well. I gave it an experimental lean to the left and squeaked loudly when the whole nest rotated with a whine. I spotted movement from the corner of my eye and looked up see that the gun turret behind was now pointing in the same direction. I pulled back on the control stick and both pairs of cannons tracked vertically. I rotated the nest back so I was facing Hoskyns. I was trying to act like a lady, but instead I was grinning like a homicidal maniac.

"Does she approve?" Mary called from below.

"I believe she does," said Hoskyns.

I stood and leaned over the edge. Mary was also failing to look like a proper grown-up.

"You did this?" I asked.

She nodded vigorously.

"I love it. I love you, too. Let us go and see about the IAG's Elephants."

"With the greatest pleasure, miss," said Hoskyns. He handed me a pair of complicated and bulky earmuffs. I inspected the things, then put them on upside-down so the headband sat under my chin. I could sense Hoskyns scowling at me. I grinned up at him.

"I don't want to ruin my hair."

"As you say, miss."

The extra machinery was jammed into where the crew spaces had been, so Hoskyns dropped through a hatch straight down to the driver's position. He left the cover open – there was going to be a lot of shouting in our future. While he trotted the elephant away from the house and in the direction of the Duneaton valley, I hacked around with my gunnery nest to see what else it would do. It wouldn't go all the way round, for one, and a full-speed traverse was quick enough to make me dizzy. I also found a skeletal bulls-eye sight folded down below the level of the hull. It didn't look like it would be much help, but I unfolded it anyway.

Hoskyns walked the elephant into a notch cut into the brow of a hill near Mennock Pass. We had a fine view of the valley curving round before us and the river running diagonally across the valley floor, but with luck we wouldn't be silhouetted against the skyline. I followed the line of the river away from us until it curved round the nearest hill and out of sight. There were sheep at the far end of a triangular patch of ground between the river and the road. As I watched, something disturbed one or two, and within moments the entire flock were pelting in the same direction. Three Steam Elephants appeared on the road where it rounded one of the far hills. Even at this distance I could see they'd been modified with wireless aerials mounted to the layered armour on each side of the driver's compartment. The burned engineering drawings I'd found at the manor suddenly made sense. The thing that was made to fit into the driver's seat was a remote control. The road continued to follow the curve of the landscape, but the Elephants ignored it and kept to their straight line. If they carried on, they'd approach our position at an angle which meant I'd have to pick them off quickly before they were too low to aim at.

"Try to get a bead on the rear one, miss," shouted Hoskyns over the turbine noise.

I lined up as best I could, adjusted for wind and gravity, and squeezed the trigger. Nothing. I swore mightily, hauled the pin with the big red ribbon that only a fool could miss from the trigger assembly and tried again.

Our Elephant shook like a team of superhuman navvies were belabouring it with railway sleepers. Four lines of fire arced over my head to explode several yards behind the trailing IAG Elephant. I swore a little more, changed my aim, and tried again. The tracer rounds spanged in all directions off the elephant, looking like particularly dangerous fireworks, but at least one of the AP rounds hit its mark because the Elephant shuddered to a halt. For a few moments, it seemed the other two would not react, but then they both cycled up to a gallop. Hoskyns was already backing us out of our hide, since we now needed to chase the remaining pair down. He took us on a path that curved down the side of the hill, following the gentler parts of the slope as much as possible. We hit the flat at the same gallop as our quarry, about halfway between them and the disabled Elephant to our rear. I'd started to line up the rearmost of the two mobile elephants when there was great thud from behind us and a pulse of disturbed air, as if someone had dropped a vicarage-sized book on a table. Shrapnel whistled past and flung great divots of mud and grass ahead of us, accompanied by rattles and clangs as flying metal hit the superstructure of our Elephant. I tried to sink lower in my nest, but there was nowhere for me to go. I just had to hope there wasn't a superheated turbine blade arcing up over the back of the Elephant ready to spear me in the stomach like a butterfly in a wooden case. I wondered if it might be better to be killed by a blow to the head and not know anything about it, rather than have to lie there and stare at the method of one's demise, quivering and ticking as it cooled while my blood leaked away and gummed up the hydraulics of the nest.

Up ahead, the remaining Elephants were approaching a bridge where a tributary of the river had been diverted through an earth covered culvert. I waited as long as I dared before sending a burst of fire a few yards ahead of the forward Elephant to crater up the approach to the bridge. I saw its gait change as the Jacquard tried to compensate for the disturbed surface, and it looked like it was going to make it, right up to the moment its right-front leg missed the bridge by a narrow margin and it lurched diagonally into the opposite bank of the river. I'd never seen a Steam Elephant crash at full speed. It hit the far bank nose-first with a noise like a locomotive hitting a crockery warehouse and began to describe great cartwheeling bounces, all flying legs and disintegrating armour plate as if thrown by an angry child. By the time the remains rattled to a halt there was nothing left to explode and I was tensing my toes in my boots as Hoskyns threaded his way through the mess I'd made of the ramp up to the bridge.

The final Elephant drew away from us. Turrets and guns were lovely things, but our Elephant was heavier and slower. I pulled back on the firing control, hoping to loft a burst in a huge arc. It was like playing with a garden hose and trying to soak an annoying cousin who was dancing about on the far side of the pea canes, convinced he was out of range. When I pressed the trigger, only half the cannons responded and a line of craters appeared well to the left of the receding elephant. I twitched the nest to the right and tried again. I was running out of time and ammunition. This fresh burst sailed at an angle low over the Elephant's back, although I thought something ricocheted off the dome of the driver's compartment. I scowled and waited until Hoskyns cleared a patch of boggy ground, then took a deep breath, re-aimed and squeezed the trigger again. Nothing but a hydraulic whine from the loading mechanism.

I thought about walloping the arm of my seat. I also wondering about bunking into the turret to swap ammunition belts around, but that would mean I'd need to learn to be an armourer and how to get into the turret from the outside of a galloping Elephant in two minutes without falling off or otherwise getting killed. Hoskyns would know, because Hoskyns seemed to know everything, but he was driving and couldn't stop because we'd lose even more ground on the remaining Elephant, which had slowed to a trot. We were close enough to see that my last burst of fire had destroyed the aerials, and without a controlling signal the elephant would... What? I ran through the sequence in my head. When our Elephant exploded it had been on the test-stand, which meant the Jacquard wasn't running anything but its idle loop. We closed rapidly on the last IAG Elephant, which had by now slowed to a walk. When it stopped, the Jacquard would begin to idle and run the code which shut down the safety valves, which would detonate the elephant just as we drew level.

"Hoskyns!"

"Miss?"

"Turn this thing round and go like the bloody clappers!"

"Miss?"

"They're guided bombs! When it stops moving, it'll go up like the one on the test stand!"

One of the many things the operations manuals for Steam Elephants caution against is trying to sharply change direction while at the gallop. I don't know what Hoskyns did, but the effect was akin to watching a speeding cat trying to corner on a polished floor. I risked a glance over the high side of the Elephant in the middle of our controlled skid to see that the other had stopped moving. We were far too close. I imagined I could hear the noise of its turbine over the noise of our own, but there was nothing I could do about any of it. I slid down in my seat and curled up as best I could while Hoskyns covered as much ground as possible.

There was another vicarage-sized thud, followed by a massive bang as something walloped our Elephant like a dinner gong for a thousand people. The poor thing went stiff-legged and juddered to a standstill as all the safety valves tripped at once, releasing a cloud of steam that enveloped us like a Turkish bath. I sat up, coughed and waved a hand in front of my face. The dark shaped that loomed at me resolved itself into Hoskyns as the steam cleared.

"Are you all right, miss?" he said.

"I need a bath and a change of clothing. And I'm not looking forward to telling Mary we broke her Elephant."

"I'm sure she'll take it in good part, miss."

My left calf felt odd. I looked down to see a turbine blade sticking sideways out of my leg.

"Bugger. I liked those boots," I said, before fainting.

#

I tried not to whimper as I descended from the train at Waverley. Hanged if I was going to wait for a porter to pitch up and hand me down from the carriage like an invalid. I made it as far as Market Street before giving in and hailing a cab.

"North side of George square, if you please," I said.

The cabbie muttered something gleefully unintelligible and steamed off up Cockburn Street with a lurch that planted me firmly in my seat.

#

It had been a painful and tedious couple of months. Yesterday I had finally managed the trip down to the end of the drive and back to St. Johnston House without having to rest, burst into tears or yell for one of the gardeners to fetch a wheelbarrow. Mary and Gerald were waiting for me as I made my way over the tricky gravel section before the semicircular stone steps that led up to the front door. I tried not to lean too hard on my stick or let on just how out of puff I was as they applauded my progress before plying me with tea and cake from the impromptu picnic laid out on the top step. They'd been gracious hosts and I'd probably been a stroppy patient.

While Hoskyns had been carrying me back to St. Johnston, Zoe and the Colonel charged another modified steam elephant into a railway siding to the north of Glasgow, stitched a long burst of tracer down the ballast to the side of the IAG excursion train, and so captured most of the group with only moderate damage to several pairs of trousers.

The discs I'd spotted at Mickleton station were the Cahill rotors, rescued from a scrapped Telharmonium in New York and shipped to the Clarendon Building as 'experimental apparatus'. They emitted a pair of Marconi beams that the equipment in the IAG elephants would track. When the rotors were shut down, or if some lucky shot destroyed the aerials on the elephants, control would be lost, the elephant would stop and the Jacquard would run the idle sequence where the halt-and-catch-fire instructions had been cut in the bogus card-books.

"... And then when Colonel Elliot had me fire another burst into the hillside behind them, they blubbed like new boys and gave up all their plans at once," Zoe said from the end of my sick-bed. "Half-baked things they were, too. Something like 'Steal elephants, some technical things, profit!' I think they'd spent so long listening to

Smith fulminate about the evils of Suffragism and women in general that they just pointed their guided elephants at Glasgow and hoped we'd get the blame."

"Us?" I squeaked.

Zoe looked daggers at the wallpaper, took a breath and then twisted on the end of the bed so she could face me without sitting on my bandage. "Us," she said. "Apparently you and I can't possibly have written either the elephant control code or a Wilkes' Analytical Language compiler, and we were taking the bread from the mouths of honest working men by pretending to do so. Presumably the Colonel and Hoskyns were among the second-rate males duped by our feminine power."

"Ha. Did you tell them who built the modified elephants?"

Zoe grinned at me. "With great glee. The look on their faces was a thing to behold."

Of Smith there had been no sign.

#

There was a brass plaque on the railings outside one of the townhouses. 'Information Retrieval Group' it read. The floor-plan in the hall directed me to the back of the building where I would find the Kernighan room.

I heard Smith's voice from three doors away. Allowing women near Jacquards would apparently bring about the ruination of the empire and right-thinking men should resist the influence of the Suffragette movement and instead work to bring about their own meritorious revolution where the worth of a man would be judged purely on contribution to the glorious future of interconnected Jacquards. I slipped as best I could through the door and took a seat at the back.

When the last of the undergraduates filed out, I made sure my stick was in plain view across my knees.

I cleared my throat.

"You have a question, Miss Butler?" Smith didn't even look up from collating his notes.

"No, Mister Smith, I do not." There was no wobble in my voice at all. Perhaps I was getting better at this adventuring business. Perhaps it was the ache in my left leg that kept my anger cold. "Instead I have a statement. Do not make any sudden movements, and please keep your hands where I can see them."

"Oh really? And what will you do if I don't?"

I twisted the handle of my stick which released the trigger with a loud click, propped it on the chair in front of me and made sure to point it at his groin.

"I shall be forced to use my little friend here. I believe the ammunition was invented by your countrymen in Detroit. Lead shot strung on piano wire. They use it as a decapitation round, but I'm sure it would be equally unpleasant when discharged at the trouser area."

Smith had the good grace to go pale, rather than bluster or threaten.

"What d'you want, Miss Butler?"

I was so tempted to smile and give him the smart answer. *So* tempted. However, this man had compromised our running code, tried to kill me twice, turned the Elephants into guided bombs and was now attempting to foment disruptive change. He was far too dangerous for me to risk being smug and careless.

"Please approach slowly. I wish to give you a leaving present."

He grinned. "I'm to be deported? Is that all?"

"In a manner of speaking, Mister Smith." I wiggled the cigarette case out of my coat pocket and lobbed it underarm the moment he was within range.

He was grinning when he caught the thing, as if the entire business was a huge practical joke on us and no hard feelings. His brow furrowed when he realised what he had in his hand. "Hey! How did you get this? This is a..."

I levered myself upright. "Say hello to the twenty-first century for me, Mister Smith."

He was still gesticulating when he faded from the timeline.

A BRISTOL POUND

by Jemma Milburn

G old flashes and darts in circles beneath the light reflecting off the water. The gurgling of the fountain, designed to be relaxing, contrasts with the noise in the shopping centre. Toby's Mum is taking ages in the stupid shops so he climbs up onto the wall to stare at the fish. The fish are much more interesting than the people pushing around him. There are smaller, stationary flashes of bronze and gold beneath the fish. Why do people pay the fish? Toby wants to pay the fish too; he'll pay them for being pretty and not boring like Mum. But he doesn't have any money. What would fish do with money anyway? They can't spend it. He could, he could spend it on sweets, like the pack he has now. Unwrapping a sweet, he decides a swapsie is probably the best thing to do.

He throws it in with a splosh and quickly reaches down to grab a coin before his Mum, or anyone else, sees. He senses grown-ups wouldn't understand the nature of the swap. Score! He gets a whole pound. Stuffing it in the little pocket in his jeans, he grins. In the car on the way home he eats another sweet and looks at the pack, there are still half of the sweets left but he feels a bit sick. He puts them away and thinks about seeing his Big Sis when they get home. She was miserable earlier when he asked if he would play with her. Mummy said it's because she's too old for playing and has studying to do, but Toby's uncle says nobody is too old for Lego. Perhaps he could give her the fishy money to buy sweets? It might cheer her up, and then she might want to play. He really wishes she would, he loves her so much, she is so clever and can do *everything*. Today he told his school friends about her doing science at college so that she'll be a scientist and that when he's old enough to go to big school he's going to join her netball team. They all got jealous and said things like "yeah well my brother has a BMX". Knowing her, though, she'd probably give this money straight back and then ignore him. He'll have to sneak it into her pocket.

\#

The graffiti on the cubicle is blurry but she's read it all before anyway. She likes being nosy about the crap other people scrawl when drunk. Who are they, what are they really like, are they just proper chavs to be doing that? Finishing her business, Natasha hunts around her body for a pen and realises she's left her handbag upstairs. She has £3.60 in her pocket. Enough for a pint, luckily. She thought she had less than that. Holding a pound coin between thumb and forefinger, she stares. At the chipboard wall, at the coin. Firmly pressing the edge of the brass into the blue paint, she etches out a message. The effort the task requires is therapeutic. Maybe somebody will read this; it's the closest anyone would get to listening. Just Imagine if she went to the bar right now and someone said, "hey, Natasha, let me buy you a drink, and I can explain the meaning of life to you!" and then they could spend all night talking of interesting things and devising a way to end wars and poverty. But what would be the point, when life is so impermanent? She takes a deep breath and rests her forehead against the cubicle wall. The taste and smell of toilet and the feel of cold damp on her skin both tell her to shift her arse out of there.

Outside the cubicle, she straightens her dress. It is pretty, blue and fashionable, Tasha is the image of a good and academic young lady. She is still holding the pound coin. Time to pucker up. In the bar, her friends are laughing and chatting at one of the big oak tables, probably still on about that geeky Sci-Fi series she's never seen. What was it – Battle Stars Galactica? She wonders if they noticed she was gone.

"A pint of Sunrise, please." She hands the money to the barman. He's quite fit, but he has dreadlocks. Probably not her type.

#

It's hot and smoggy today, and Neil knots his dreadlocks at the back of his head to keep his neck cool. He checks he has enough cash, and politely shakes his head at the Big Issue seller who shouts "God Bless You" at him. Nice guy, he's always upbeat and shaking people's hands, knows half the neighbourhood, by face at least. Not today. The little Hallal shop doesn't take card. Neil is picking up some shopping for his next door neighbour. She's tired and busy with five grandchildren to look after during the day. She deserves whatever feast she will cook up tonight. He knows she'll serve herself last. He doesn't have a family himself but can imagine how stressful it might be. Then again, it's probably worth it, maybe someday, with the right girl. After paying and packing, he buys some kateyef for one pound and hides it among the shopping in the bag as a surprise.

#

Paul nips into the nearest shop, ducking so his Mohawk fits under the doorway. It took half an hour to do this morning, longer than usual with the colour still coming out. It is absolutely solid with sugar. He barely looks around, it's like a convenience store except it has a meat counter. He approaches the guy at the till.

" 'Scuze, have you got change for a tenner, mate?"

The shop assistant looks sulky, but obliges.

"Thanks."

Stepping back outside, Paul hands five pounds to his mate in exchange for the fags he bought earlier. He takes one out for himself and lights up.

His mate waves his own smouldering fag in a goodbye gesture. "See you at the Junction."

A load of local punk bands are playing there later, mediocre, but that's what it's all about, hanging out, seeing mates. Paul puts his earphones in. Discharge, he's had an appetite for hardcore lately. He turns the volume up loud. What the hell, he's half deaf anyway. He strides toward the Bear Pit for his daily fix, chains clinking against studs, leather creaking. He scratches at his bad skin and thinks about how he's got to get fitter. If you want to make any changes in the world, you've got to start with yourself. In the subway that connects the bottom of the M32 to the rest of the city he heads straight towards his new mate. He's a regular customer now. After all, you can't beat getting all five of your daily fruit and veg for £1.

#

The fruit and veg man passes the pound in change straight to another customer. Dean is in a flap, trying to shop with two kids, a pushchair and a changing bag hanging off his arm. His two-year-old son is whinging because he's too hot, and he's disturbing his baby sister. Dean packs the veg under the pram. He wants to meet his wife for lunch; she's working late tonight so it would be nice for her to see the kids now.

"Come on kids, Mummy's waiting."

There is a canteen on the top floor of the office. Dean hasn't been here before, but he's been told that it welcomes families. He gets a tray and selects orange juice and grapes for the kids, and orders two fresh coffees. The kids finally shut up, snuggled on their Mum's arm and smiling up at her like a pair of angels, like they've never had a tantrum in their lives.

"How's your morning been, darling?" his wife asks.

"It's been good, thanks. We had a play in the sand pit and Daddy did some cleaning." He smiles ruefully. "I've promised to buy a paddling pool for this heat, and we did a bit of shopping on the way here." He stretches, fingers linked to cradle the back of his head against his palms, looking down at his wife. She really is gorgeous, she looks so professional in her suit today, relaxing with the kids. He can't wait to snuggle up in bed with her tonight.

"Oh, Boo! What have you got there?" She darts forward, a look of terror on her face. "Dean, get it off her, she'll choke!"

Dean's baby girl is grinning. Gold glints in her mouth, the pound coin, his change from the veg stall. How the hell did she get hold of that?

"Come here darling." He coaxes her mouth open. "Let Daddy have it, taaa!"

Reluctantly Boo yields up her treasure, sticky with saliva.

"I'm going to buy your mummy some chocolate on the way home with that for tonight." He smiles at his wife, wiping the coin on his jeans and stashing it in his pocket. She gives him a frosty glare and resumes drinking her lukewarm coffee. He'd do anything for her.

#

George nips into the garage and considers the Galaxy chocolate on special offer, £1 for a big bar. He came in for two cups of coffee – black, no sugar – his beat mate tonight is too much like himself. Still adjusting from his change of shift he yawns and stretches, wincing as his shirt rubs his sunburn. Bad idea, laying the new drive yesterday with no top on. The woman behind the counter is lush, he always has had a thing for redheads. But she's likely working too late to go out on the town tonight. Probably a good thing, He has seen many an attractive person turn ugly come three in the morning. He hands over a fiver with a smile and a polite word of thanks, and slips the pound change loose into his right pocket. He wonders if tonight will have any particular dramas.

Inevitably there are people staggering about, illegal street sellers with plastic roses and sparkly cowboy hats he gently but firmly encourages to move on, various drug incidents. He ignores the marijuana – what's the point? It would only lead to yet more paperwork, plus he hates being a hypocrite. Some men are getting leery outside the Commercial Rooms. George steps in to break up the trouble and gets shoved by a burly drunk. He break-rolls onto his right hip to avoid injury and springs back to his feet. His partner steps in but George is already on the guy, pinning the man with his arm twisted behind his back. He's spitting and cursing his way into more serious trouble. No big deal, just one more for a cell tonight. Later he sits in the van, flicking through Zoo, but he doesn't really look at the women. He thinks he might train in a second martial art, maybe Karate. As the earth spins back into dawn-light and hides its uglier face in shadow, the people crawl back into their holes, closing curtains and slamming windows to shut out the dawn chorus. George will head home to have dinner while his girlfriend eats her breakfast.

#

Mic cuts off the tune he's whistling when he realises it's the theme to Thomas the Tank Engine. That stupid toy in the conservatory went off with its little tune again last night. Probably the cat setting it off, he'll chuck her out tonight. It's a beautiful Saturday morning. He spots something glinting in the gutter outside the closed pub, and with a groan he bends to pick it up.

"Here look mate, I've found a quid!"

"Easiest quid you've ever earned, mate," his friend replies.

Mic smiles to himself. Today will be good. It's his day off and he's lucky.

"Can you spare any change, please?"

Mic shrugs and tosses the coin, which clinks into the polystyrene cup of a skinny young man huddled in a doorway.

"What did you do that for?" his companion asks.

"I dunno, feeling generous I guess. Why not?"

"I tell you why not – what do you think *he's* going to spend that on now. . . ?"

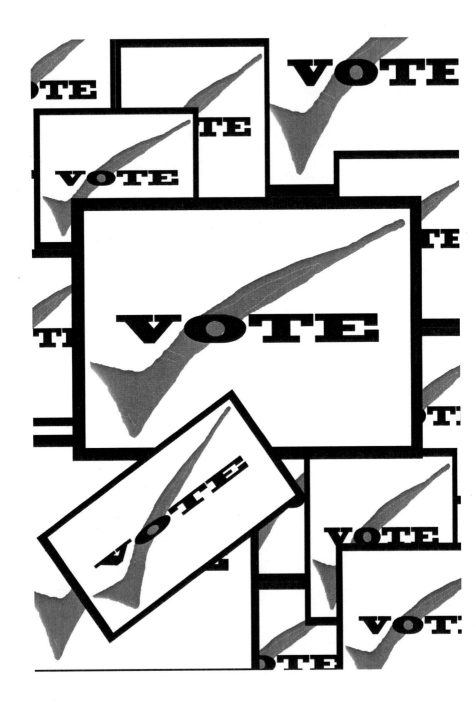

LYE CLOSE

By Ian Millsted

T *oo many people.* Martin looked around at the campaign HQ. It
was the usual problem. Given the opportunity the volunteers
always gravitated to where there were chairs, tea and biscuits and,
most importantly, other people to chat to or chat up. There were
people here from London, Manchester (mainly a party from the
university) and even Sunderland; ostensibly to go and campaign for
the party but half of them had arrived only to take root, it seemed.
Today was day one of a twenty-five day campaign and he expected
to do what he was about to do at least fifty times before polling day.
He stepped up on a chair and raised his voice.

"Anybody who is not called Muriel and is sat inputting canvas
returns to the computer should be out there getting people to
bloody well vote for Terry. And I include myself. Pick up a pile of
newsletters and a Bristol A to Z from the trestle table below the pin
board and get delivering."

As the last of the volunteers hit the pavements, Martin grabbed
a pile of newsletters, noting the street name, and headed out. He
lived for this. He loved the sense of doing something where he knew
he could be effective. He'd run campaigns at university and been
a volunteer himself at the previous general election and any by-
election he could get to since. For the last two years he had been a
paid agent here in Bristol working to overturn the modest majority
of the government M.P. He was confident. Terry was a decent, if
not particularly flamboyant, candidate and the last round of local
election results had pointed the right way, but he knew well enough
not to take anything for granted. What he could do was make sure

every house was visited and every possible voter spoken to. The volunteers might find him annoying today but he'd buy them drinks tonight while they exchanged stories to see who had encountered the fiercest dog or maddest voter.

The list of addresses he had took him an hour and a half to finish. He was on his way back when he met Bob and Juliet, who had come across from Bath where the party wasn't putting in much of a campaign. Bob waved a sheet of paper and his phone in the air.

"Got a funny one here, Martin. We've got one address listed for Lye Close. It's not in the A to Z but it's on Google maps. We've walked round where it's supposed to be but we can't find the road, let alone the house. Only one voter listed. Should we bother?"

"Probably not worth the time, but I'll have a look anyway. Chase every vote."

Bob smiled as he handed over the details, pleased to be done for the morning.

#

Martin found Lye Close exactly where Google Maps indicated it should be. He made a pencil correction on the A to Z. No wonder the party barely registered in Bath if their members couldn't even find a street this easy. The road was short and mostly made up of the backs of gardens to houses on neighbouring roads. The one house accessed via the close was tucked away in a corner; a small, modern detached house with, probably, three bedrooms. Martin tried to guess the resident type. Maybe an underpaid, lower level lecturer from the University. He hoped so, anyway – they were often sympathetic.

He rang the doorbell and waited, listening for sounds from within. After a decent interval, he rang again and started folding up a 'sorry you were out' leaflet, when the door opened.

"Yes?"

He guessed the woman to be in her mid twenties. She smiled in a friendly enough way. All she wore was a towel wrapped around her, leaving her shoulders and legs bare. Martin introduced himself in the usual way. He made a conscious effort to smile, make eye contact and not look any lower than her neck.

"Oh, thanks," the woman said. "Sorry to come to the door like this, but I was just getting out of the shower when you rang. Put me down as a probable supporter. My name's Jenny, but you've probably got that on your list anyway. Better go, I don't want to stand in the doorway like this."

Martin made a written note of her voting inclination and a mental note to call back some time to further persuade her.

#

Twenty days to go. Most of the student volunteers had left with promises that they would be back for the last week. *We'll see.* He didn't care much. They'd been hard work to organise and he was in a good mood having seen the latest internal polling figures. Delivering a new set of leaflets which headlined Terry's background in the NHS, Martin found himself near Lye Close again. *Well, she did say she was only probable.*

"Hi," she said. "Come in. I'm decent this time. I was sorry to hear about the result."

What? "I'm sorry, did you say result?"

"And so close too. Must be frustrating."

Martin mumbled a vague acknowledgement.

"To be honest, I think if you'd been the candidate, you would have won," Jenny said. "You come over well on the doorstep."

"Something to think about," Martin replied, backing down the drive in mild confusion.

#

Fourteen days to go. He had mostly been too busy to think about Jenny or Lye Close. One vote in a street wasn't worth any more of an investment in time. The canvas returns had started to show things getting tighter so all his waking hours were spent talking to voters and the media. But in what should have been his non-waking hours he found himself thinking about the strange, possibly mad, woman in Lye Close who seemed to think she knew the result already.

When he found himself walking into Lye Close anyway, after dropping leaflets nearby, he told himself it was because of an attractive woman who answered the door in nothing but a towel, and that she must have been joking about the result.

"It's you," she said, even while the door was still swinging open. "Congratulations. See, I told you it would go better if you stood yourself. I'm surprised to see you though – I thought you'd be on your way to London by now."

Martin thanked her for her support and accepted the offer of a coffee. She led him through to the lounge and went off to make the coffee. The room was warm, comfortable and uncluttered. There was no calendar on view, nor any newspapers or anything that might indicate the date.

"I was wondering," he said when she returned with two cups of coffee on a tray, "where do you get your news from?"

"Radio mostly, or internet. No T.V. though. I'm away a lot and tend to keep a simple house, but I made sure I was here to vote." She smiled as she sat at the opposite end of the sofa, crossing her legs so one foot pointed towards him. "So, what's the first thing you're going to do now you're elected?"

What year is this? He kept wanting to ask the question, but somehow the words wouldn't come.

#

Seven days to go. The numbers were too close to call. Terry tried to blame him for the campaign stalling. They had a blazing row, and Martin told Terry exactly what he thought of him as a public speaker, and Terry stormed out.

These things happened in elections. It would be alright once they won, but Martin needed to be somewhere away from the rest of the team while he calmed down.

Once again he rang the doorbell of the house in Lye Close. The first thing he noticed was that she had been to the hairdressers and had a restyle, sometime in the last week. He told her he liked it, and she gave him a bemused look.

"Congratulations again. Increased majority. No surprise really. I see they're tipping you for a job in government."

Martin let Jenny speak, interjecting with only the occasional neutral response. He declined the offer of a coffee this time. She was wearing more make-up and he suspected, with a pang of jealousy, that she was ready to go out with someone for the evening.

#

Three days to go. Martin had stopped looking at the canvas returns. He could tell what he needed to know from people's faces. He and Terry had made their apologies to each other. The national campaign was going well, but news from other marginals was mixed.

Martin stood at the end of Lye Close for several minutes, wondering why he was there again, and what was he going to say.

"Back again," Jenny said, with a soft smile. "Must be an election in the offing. I hope what they're saying about you isn't true. I wouldn't want to think I voted for someone like that." She winked at him. "A sex scandal I could live with, but money, well...you never seemed that type."

"I'd be very interested in hearing your views."

She shared them with him, quite clearly and at some length.

#

The morning after. What was it she had said? "So close". Twenty three votes close. He'd been in to the campaign HQ. No one was there. Most of the bottles of sparkling wine they'd got in to celebrate with had gone, but taken away unopened to be drunk later. No one had been popping corks last night.

He walked the streets for something to do, knowing that his footsteps would take him once more to Lye Close.

She didn't invite him in, but she looked at him with sad, older looking, eyes. "I'm sorry you lost, I really am."

She said more but he didn't hear most of it. He thanked her, and walked away.

About the story

The existence, or non-existence, of Lye Close was something I first found out about from Eugene Byrne. It exists, as the story says, on Google maps but nowhere else. It is a copyright protection mechanism; a deliberate mistake that can prove material has been stolen. It suggested itself for one of those fictional places that slip in and out of reality. Of course the idea of something being presented as real when there is no substance and the political slant of the story have absolutely no connection at all!

NORTH BY SOUTHWEST

CHRISTMAS STEPS

By Pete Sutton

There was a stabbing on Christmas Steps. We were both there. It was foggy and dark, but with that orange penumbral glow you get from the streetlights. I walked past St Bartholomew's, thinking about electric monks as I usually do when passing that cloaked horseman statue. The artist, David Backhouse, said the statue is of no particular person but represents 'a reminder of people from the past', which seemed appropriate. He also said his art 'is about the way in which nature and humans depend on one another and the search for balance and harmony' which sounded like arty wank to me.

I wondered what it would be like if all the statues in the city were sentient. It would be OK for the ones that had other statues nearby to converse silently with, but it would be terribly lonely for those like the horseman. I wondered about his thoughts as he sat watching the road traffic alternately crawling or zooming past, or the random wandering of shoppers and revellers.

You were walking down Park Row. The scent of fish and chips only partly masked the muffling wet dog smell of the fog. You were probably thinking of going home, of dinner or something else mundane. I was constructing a new fantasy in my head, as usual, wondering what the collective noun for statues was. I was disappointed to find that the Wikipedia entry on collective nouns didn't have statues. It had a 'rout of snails' and a 'scurry of squirrels' and a 'trip of stoats', but nothing related to statues. Perhaps I should invent one? A stillness of statues, a silence of statues, a freeze of statues perhaps, or a pondering of statues since they must think deep thoughts. These musings brought me to the bottom of the steps. I checked the Bristol Culture webpage again to start me off.

'In medieval times, the Christmas Steps was [should that be were?] called Queene Street, later becoming known as Knyfesmyth Street after its specialist traders. At its foot for centuries was a statue of the Madonna and child, rubbed smooth by generations of people for luck. The beheaded statue can still be seen just inside the entrance to St Bartholomew's Court.' Would beheaded or disarticulated statues have their own collective noun? The iconoclasts defaced statues – the Taliban famously blew up the Buddhas of Bamiyan. So an effacement of effigies, perhaps?

I was researching a story about a stabbing. I was going to set it on Knyfesmyth Street. It would be about a young man, younger than me, maybe your age He comes to rub the statue of the Madonna and child for luck. He's annoyed a powerful criminal and men are coming for him, the kind of men I'm probably going to describe as burly. I could also describe them as utterly barking and very dangerous. I wonder what thoughts swirled around your head as you approached the top of the steps. I wondered, at the time, what thoughts would swirl around the head of my young man as he looked for some supernatural aid. Was he a true believer, or did the smoothly rubbed statue hold some particular meaning for him? Perhaps he had noted the statue previously whilst shopping for a knyfe? Or perhaps I should develop a scene with a small beggar girl who tells him of the magic contained within the statue and how it saved her from some dread disease of the street? Perhaps I should have a 'fighting of beggars', since I'm still thinking of collective nouns and that's such a good one. I wonder if the horseman, or someone like him, sat pondering whilst believers rubbed the statue.

You were silhouetted at the top of the steps and I assume I must have been the same at the bottom. I only half looked at you, as I was looking at the steps and making mental notes whilst paying too much attention to my phone. You paused, then started down the well-worn route trodden by many over the centuries. I stood, lost in thought, wondering about the specialist knife merchants who used to occupy the street. I wondered how many synonyms for knife there actually are and which would fit my story best. A dimly glinting dagger perhaps, or a wickedly thin dirk; possibly I should be alliterative; a cruel cleaver, a strident stiletto... maybe not. One to play with later, I guessed.

Was it an opportunity for you? Did you think I was someone else? People often do; I've been told I have one of those faces that make people think they know me. Did you catch the tenuous half-shaped story as it flitted up and down the stairs, or was that only visible to me? Perhaps it caught you and you sleepwalked through actions given fleeting form in the fog. You made your approach and I finally became fully aware of you and thought about how I should walk up the steps now. My writer's glance worked to categorize you and add to my young man at the same time. Your dark ski jacket becoming an oilskin in my imagination, your baseball cap more time-appropriate headgear as I tried different shapes in my imagination. You looked straight at me and I wonder what you saw. Possibly all you focussed on was my dreamy but intense gaze, illuminated by the screen of my phone. Perhaps you'd had a bad night, perhaps you were angry at the world, perhaps you were high, perhaps you spotted an opportunity, perhaps I had unknown mortal enemies that had paid for an assassin, perhaps you were an escapee from a secure mental institution. I am left with a plethora of perhapses.

I thought a knife would glint but perhaps there was no fog in my story. I had thought my burly fellows would grunt as they stabbed, but you emitted no sound. You slashed and stabbed so quickly as the fog rolled down the steps and matched the fog of pain that closed my eyes as you ran away, my phone in your hand, your footsteps sounding uncannily slow to my wildly beating heart. At least now I'll be able to describe what it feels like to be stabbed, I think, as the world becomes ever more foggy and my eyes start to close.

The slow metallic clop of the pale horse and its rider approaching. David Backhouse was wrong about what his work represented. I wasn't wrong though, he does look lonely. A clever bird lands close by and gives me a sceptical glance, I wonder if there is a collective noun for psychopomps.

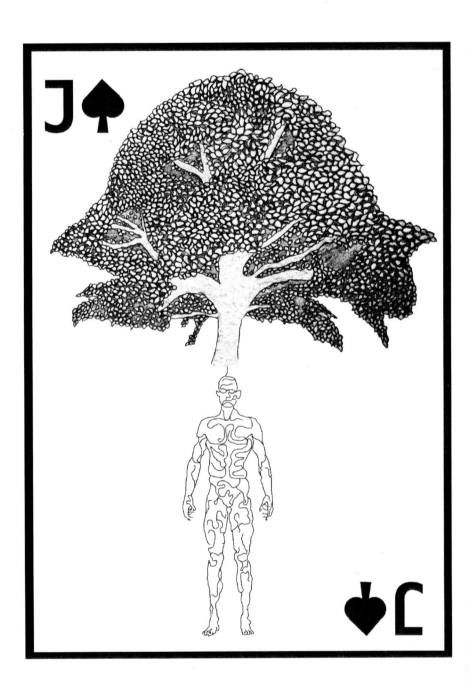

GARDENING LEAVE

By Clare Dornan

He stood at the window, motionless except for his fingers, which drummed a gentle rhythm on the window ledge. Outside in the darkness, the trees bent precariously before the force of the wind. The heavy rain was flooding the roads, the gutters overflowing with the icy onslaught. Cars crept past, windscreen wipers barely able to clear the screen.

He turned away from the window and sat at his desk, staring into the blackness that surrounded him. His hands clenched neatly in front of him.

Do I really need to finish this? he thought. *Have I not done enough?*

He switched on the gold desk lamp and pulled a set of keys from his pocket. He flicked through them, one by one, until he found the small key that unlocked the bottom drawer of his desk. The drawer was crammed with black leather-bound diaries with the years etched in gold on the front covers. He pushed them aside, reaching deep into the drawer to find what he was looking for. It was hidden at the bottom, right at the back. A small pack of playing cards.

He slipped the cards out of their case and shuffled them methodically, splitting the pack and sliding the two halves together. Then he began to lay out the cards on the smooth leather surface of his desk, the rhythmic flick, flick, flick of the cards breaking the silence of the room.

He paused and picked up the last card in the line, holding it under the lamp to illuminate the design.

The Ace of Clubs: the Willow Tree.

His eyes closed and his head dropped forward, as if he slept. His hand, clutching the card, fell to his lap and his thumb gently stroked the surface.

At length, he raised his head. He slipped the Ace into his pocket, pushed wearily to his feet and returned to the window, to watch the storm batter the street below.

\#

Jenny drew up and parked outside Trinity Road in a space normally taken by one of her more punctual colleagues. She strode down the corridor into the heart of the building, shrugging her coat off her shoulders as she neared her office. Her boss, Chief Superintendent David Ross raised an eyebrow in surprise at her arrival, and checked his watch.

"I thought there would be traffic chaos after last night," she said. "I decided to set off early for a change."

She joined Ross by the small kitchen area as he reached for two mugs from the shelf above.

"What's the latest?" she asked, filling the mugs with freshly brewed coffee.

"The storm damage is extensive along the water front and the Portway is still flooded this morning. Hardy has more details," he said. "Apart from that, it's generally quiet. Nothing for you to get in on time for."

That was one advantage of bad weather. No one liked being out in the pouring rain – the number of burglaries, car thefts and drunken fights were always reduced when the weather closed in.

She sat at her desk in the corner of the main office. Her computer was still grinding into life when Will Jackson strode into the room. He placed his cycling helmet and jacket on the desk next to hers. "You're early," he said with his usual wide smile. "I thought you'd have a nightmare getting across town."

"You haven't missed anything vital – just the storm debris to sort through," she said, blowing gently on her coffee, the steam fogging her glasses. She pushed a pile of papers to one side to make space for the cup, next to two half-empty mugs from the day before.

The office filled with noise and activity as the team arrived and further reports of storm damage came in. A call came through about a suspected looting at a shop in Hotwells and Jenny had her coat in hand, ready to drive to the scene, when her phone rang. The duty officer on the front desk cut straight to the point.

"I've got a Mr Alfred Cooper on the line, who says he works at Long Grove mansion. He asked to speak to you personally – shall I connect you?"

"Put him through." The name was familiar. Alfred Cooper obviously knew her, but Jenny racked her brain for the connection, and came up blank. No doubt it would come back to her as they talked. Whoever he was, Alfred Cooper sounded agitated, with a tremor in his voice that was more than just age.

"DI Bradley? You came to talk to us some time ago about security on the estate. I still have your card. I thought it best to call you directly."

Jenny sat back down at her desk, her coat ruffling the papers on her desk. "It's no trouble, Mr Cooper. Is there a problem with the house?"

"No, no, the house is fine. That's all fine, but the trees, the trees are uprooted everywhere. There's terrible damage to the grounds. It's awful just awful…"

"I can imagine," she said, gently, worried for the old man. Was he in that big house all alone? He sounded vulnerable. "And how can I help you, Mr Cooper?"

"Oh God, I've never seen anything like it. One of the great oaks came down in the storm. I went to see it, and when I got back down the hill I found your card and phoned you straight away. You've got to come. I don't know what it is."

"Mr Cooper, can you explain what's happened?"

"It's in the roots, it's underground. There's someone down there. There's a body under the tree."

#

Will drove them out of town while Jenny sat staring out of the window at the city flashing by, trying to recall her last visit to Long Grove. The huge country estate on the outskirts of the city had at its heart an imposing Georgian mansion. The building had once been the country residence of a rich Bristol merchant, but it was now a business centre and popular wedding venue. Every summer weekend, brides and grooms could be seen posing for photos on its impressive marble steps.

The car turned off the main road. A 'closed to the public' sign blocked the entrance, but the gates to the main drive were unlocked. They followed the line of tall birch trees directly to the front entrance of the main house. The landscape rolled away in all directions with open grassland and, in the distance, forested hills. The public areas of the estate were popular with walkers during the summer months, but on a stormy Sunday night in March no one in their right mind would be out exploring the woods.

Cooper's agitation had clearly been exacerbated by his wait for their arrival. Before they had time to get out of the car, he was hovering nervously at Jenny's door.

"We need to walk through the field, and up the far hill," he said, the instant she stepped out of the car.

"That's not a problem." Jenny fastened her long cream coat around her. "Mr Cooper, this is my colleague, Sergeant Jackson."

Cooper gave him a brief nod, and accepted his handshake.

"Is the owner of the house around?" Jenny asked. The frown on Albert Cooper's face deepened.

"He's in the Caribbean. I haven't been able to contact him. I've left messages, but I don't know when he'll get them."

"It's best we talk to as few people as possible at this stage." Jenny indicated for Cooper to lead the way. "At least until we know what we're dealing with."

They set off across the damp grass, littered with leaves and debris from the storm, and entered the edge of the wood. Cooper's quick nervous pace left Will and Jenny struggling up the slope in his wake.

"It's over the other side of the hill. A bit of a climb, I'm afraid."

"How did you come across it?" Jenny asked as she caught up with him. Her heavy breaths steamed in the chill morning air. "It seems to be on a very remote part of the grounds."

"You're right, it's not part of the public area. I don't often get over here, but there are more old trees in this corner than anywhere else. I wanted to see if they survived the storm."

As they reached a clearing, Cooper's pace slackened. Ahead, the sprawling branches of the fallen oak, still fluttering with the first leaves of spring, stretched out across the ground to meet them. His steps faltered and he froze, just beyond the reach of the trailing branches.

Jenny placed a hand on his shoulder and nodded to Will to accompany her. They walked down the length of the tree to where it had been ripped out of the ground, leaving a damp, muddy hole and bare roots stretching to the sky. At the bottom of the hole, an arm stretched up to greet them, grey skin coated with mud.

She felt the shock jerk through her body and she stepped back crashing into Will who was frozen to the spot behind her. He lifted his hands to steady her, but his eyes never left the single hand with its fingers curled into a claw.

"We're going to need forensics here straight away," Jenny said, fumbling in vain for her phone, trying to sound far more controlled than she felt.

"I'll call them now," Will said. "My phone's here." He stepped back from the grave site.

Jenny exhaled deeply and rummaged in her bag for a pair of latex gloves. She snapped them on and reached out for the cold hand. She squeezed the flesh. It had a strange dry texture that reminded her of meat that had defrosted and refrozen once too often.

She felt instantly sure of two things. That this person had died long before last night's storm, probably months ago by the rate of decomposition, and that their death had been no accident.

As she stood back from the body, it struck her how quiet it was. They were too far from any roads to hear even the faintest hum of traffic. The person who had buried this body would have known this was a quiet spot, where things could be hidden and lay undisturbed for years.

Cooper was standing with his back to the fallen tree, looking out across the clearing. When Jenny put her hand on his shoulder, she realised he was still shaking.

"It's a beautiful spot, don't you think?" he said, speaking so quietly his voice was barely a whisper. A mist was forming low over the grass, illuminated by the weak spring sunshine. "Maybe they loved this place so much, they wanted to stay here?" He turned towards her, his eyes glinting. "Is that what you think too, Detective Bradley?"

She sensed his desperation; he needed her reassurance that this peaceful spot hadn't born witness to a violent death, but it was a reassurance she couldn't provide.

#

Four hours later, and the peace of the wood had been utterly shattered. A white tent covered the grave site and the Forensic team was painstakingly extricating the body from its resting place.

Jenny looked up as the buzz of the press helicopters rumbled overhead. The vultures were already circling and they would be feasting on this for weeks.

She pulled her phone from her pocket and called Chief Superintendent Ross.

"What have you got so far?" he asked sharply.

"It's a male, slim build, I'd guess late thirties. No wallet or ID found so far and no clear sign of how he died. They'll move him out in the next hour or so and take him to the coroners for the full autopsy."

"OK, I'll set an investigation team up here. Hardy will be running this one. Call in and update everyone this afternoon."

Jenny grew cold. "Chief? I imagined this would continue to be my investigation. Why is Hardy in charge?"

"As my most senior detective..."

"I'm more than capable of running this investigation," Jenny interrupted "I don't..."

"This is not up for discussion, Bradley." The phone clicked off, leaving Jenny staring at the screen in disbelief. DI Hardy was no slouch, but he was hardly dynamic, and this was likely to be the biggest case they had all year. He was a gruff, overbearing man, practical but unimaginative. He had worked alongside the Chief for years as a solid, unchallenging presence.

Now he had been rewarded for his plodding detective work with the best case they'd had for months. *Her* case.

\#

At the car park, Jenny could see Will was still inside Cooper's office where he had been interviewing the staff and collecting details on the estates past employees. She leaned on the car, smoking a cigarette to calm her anger, and trying to resist the urge to bite her nails. She stared across the estate, to where the yellow police tape marked the edge of the search area. How could the Chief have given her case to that dullard Hardy? What the hell was going on?

She looked up as she heard the door to Cooper's office close. Will was walking towards the car, lugging an apparently heavy box of paperwork. He offered an awkward shrug.

"Five years worth of casual employees, and apparently our Mr Cooper doesn't like computers…" He trailed off. "What's wrong with you?"

"Are you good to go?" She threw the cigarette on to the floor and ground it into the gravel. "You'll need to get those back for Hardy and his team to work on."

Will looked at her quizzically.

"Hardy? What are you talking about? That's not possible."

"I'm afraid it is. Chief Ross just called. He's given the case to Hardy. I'm to brief him when we get back."

Will frowned and shifted the hefty box into the boot.

"But I'm serious, that's not possible," he said. "Hardy's going in for a hernia operation at the end of the week. He won't be in work for a while."

Jenny stared at him in disbelief. "Are you sure? How do I not know that? And why doesn't the Chief?"

"If you ever came to the pub after work, you'd hear more of the gossip." Will grinned. "He's been keeping it quiet, but I'm surprised the Chief didn't speak to Hardy before he told you."

Jenny shook her head in confusion. It was not like the Chief to make such a clumsy mistake. Will was obviously mulling over the same idea.

"The press will be all over this one. Maybe he wanted Hardy to be the one in front of the cameras."

"What's that supposed to mean? Are you saying I can't deal with the press?" She slammed the car door behind her with considerable venom. Will, wisely, let the subject drop.

#

When they arrived back at the station, Jenny left Will to park and bounded up the stairs, heading straight for the Chief's office. Before she reached the door, it opened and Chief Superintendent Ross stepped out into the corridor in front of her.

"Sir, I didn't mean to question your decision earlier, but I do feel I have the necessary experience to run this investigation. I've worked closely with press before --"

"It turns out Hardy has leave booked that I wasn't aware of," the Chief interrupted.

Jenny felt the wind had been whipped neatly from her sails. "Oh," she managed. "Oh, I see."

Ross lowered his head and paused. Jenny was momentarily struck by the impeccably neat parting in his hair. In fact everything was always precise and thorough with him. It was one of the things she admired about him. It made his rash decision about Hardy even more bizarre.

"So, he won't be available to front this case?"

"No, he will not."

"So do I have your permission to continue?"

He looked at her dispassionately.

"Yes, carry on, Bradley." He gestured for her to lead the way back to the investigation room.

The team of eight officers were already gathered for the briefing. Jenny glanced towards Will as she entered with Ross and gave him a smile and a discreet thumbs up.

She walked to the front of the room and turned to the assembled team.

"As you've all heard, we've got an unidentified white male, approximately six foot, slim build and estimated to be in his late thirties. He was found this morning in the grounds of the Long Grove estate. The body was buried approximately half a metre underground, within the roots of a large tree. Last night the tree was felled in the storm, which led to the discovery of the body this morning.

The forensic team are on location and at present their analysis on the state of decomposition suggests he's been there for between one and two years. We will get a more detailed timeframe after the full autopsy."

"Our first aim is to identify him. I need all missing persons reports gathered that fit the description so far – let's start within the city and then broaden the search area. Have there been any reports of suspicious behaviour, any complaints lodged in the area in the past couple of years? I know this was probably some time ago but maybe someone remembers seeing something unusual."

Chief Superintendent Ross cleared his throat.

"There will be a press conference in two hours time, at five pm. I don't need to remind everyone that there will be no leaking of information to the press during this investigation. We will temporarily be in the national spotlight, so let's keep this tight and wrap it up quickly."

The team returned to their desks and the Chief hurried out of the office without a word to Jenny. She was pleased to be in charge, but shaken by the Chief's lack of faith in her. She had always been under the impression he thought highly of her. An impression she now feared she had totally misjudged.

#

Jenny's footsteps echoed in the clinical hallway outside the coroner's office. She knocked, took a deep breath and entered the autopsy room.

"Thank you for coming, detective" the coroner said quietly, not looking up from his notes.

Jenny approached the white cloth-covered body on the table beside him. The coroner looked up, watching her intently as her hand hovered over the cloth for a moment before she let it fall.

"I'm Jenny Bradley. I've only been in Bristol for a year, and yes, before you ask, I've seen dead bodies before."

He returned her smile. "Excellent," he said, "It's always good to see a new face."

He seemed upbeat considering his line of work and Jenny had an inkling of what that meant. He'd found something unusual.

He reached for his notes and skimmed through his report. "Cause of death is a sharp impact to the top of the neck – looks like a neat blow – maybe one or two hits. Decomposition is fairly advanced – impossible to get fingerprints as there's too much tissue damage. DNA from his hair follicles was sent through to the lab last night." He put his notes down and pulled back the sheet to uncover the corpse.

"I would say he has been underground for at least two years," he continued. "There's plenty of evidence of insect activity. Our forensic entomologist inspected a number of larval egg cases and concludes the body was buried shortly after being killed, as the cases are from beetles that like fresh flesh – and also that he was killed in spring due to the amount of beetle activity. There would be far fewer in winter, more in the summer time."

Jenny nodded. "Anything that could help identification?"

"Well, I can tell you he was a heavy smoker and he didn't have an appendix. But," he paused, and she sensed this was what he had been waiting to tell her, "the strangest thing wasn't in his body, but what was stuck to him."

"Stuck to him?"

The coroner reached for a small clear plastic bag and passed it to her. Inside was a single water-stained playing card. On one side was the Jack of Clubs, on the other a picture of an oak tree.

"He was found under an oak tree." she said quietly, and the coroner said nothing, but his single raised eyebrow said it all.

#

With the card in her pocket, Jenny drove back to the station. The news on the radio gave the unidentified body in Bristol top billing and included a request for information from the public. The news dissolved into the latest sport updates and Jenny reached over to silence it. The discovery of the card would have to be kept quiet for now – at least until they knew what it meant.

As she left the car her phone lit up. She answered it without breaking stride, and walked straight into the office to find Ross quizzing the team. She wanted to remonstrate with him for interfering in her case, but in her ear, the lab was running through the results of the DNA test.

She interrupted the Chief as he was mid-question.

"Sir, we have a name – his DNA is in the database. Our body is a Charles Hemon."

The team's reaction was sudden and unexpected. The sense of

surprise was palpable. The Chief reddened and spluttered. "Charles Hemon?"

"Yes sir, that's what they said. Long record of burglary, breaking and entering..."

"Yes, thank you, Detective," the Chief snapped. "I'm aware of Mr Hemon's previous misdemeanours. What I want to know," his eyes narrowed and angry, "is if Charles Hemon has been fertilizing a bloody oak tree in Long Grove for the last two years, then why the hell have I just submitted an extradition order to get him back from Spain?"

A silence fell over the room. The Chief rubbed his thumb across his forehead, ironing out the frown between his eyes. He looked deflated as he turned back to the door of his private office. He paused and everyone waited for him to speak. When he did his voice was subdued; the passion had ebbed away.

"Detective Bradley, could I see you for a minute, please?" he said, before disappearing into his room.

Under the watchful gaze of her team, Jenny followed him in. The Chief stood by the window, gazing into the car park below. He signalled for her to take a seat.

"It's a bloody mess," he said, some of his ire returning. "A right bloody mess."

"Sir, with respect, we have an identification already. We have a good team on this. It's a mess that can be resolved."

His face was closed, his expression one she couldn't read, until a small resigned smile flickered briefly across his lips.

"Fine. You're in charge of this investigation, but you need to talk to Hardy before he disappears for this bloody operation."

He picked up his phone and spoke to Hardy's secretary.

"He can meet you now in his office. If it really is Charlie Hemon under that tree, then there's a lot about the Hemons you need to know."

"Sir, before I go, there's something you should see." Jenny retrieved the clear plastic bag from her pocket. "The coroner found it under his clothes. It looks like it was deliberately buried with the body."

The Chief took the specimen bag and peered at the oak tree design on the card.

"He was found under an oak tree, sir," she said. "I can't think this is a coincidence."

"No," he said, turning the card over and holding it up to the light. "No, you're probably right." He handed it back with a nod. "Go and see Hardy now. Let him fill you in about the Hemons."

#

Jenny didn't know Hardy well. She knew he was a bore, and a plod, and that he'd almost stolen the investigation that might make her career. The only other thing she knew about him was that, like her, he avoided social work gatherings and preferred to keep his private life separate from the office. That didn't mean they had anything in common.

She knocked at his door and heard his harsh bark for entry.

Hardy already knew the outline of the case, but his surprise at the discovery of Charlie Hemon mirrored that of the Chief.

"We've been after the little bugger for months on outstanding drug charges. We sometimes get reports of him accessing his bank accounts from Spain, so we thought he was sunning himself down on the south coast. Recently the Spanish police arrested a man called Charlie Hemon and an extradition order is in to get his sorry arse back here. How much do you know about the Hemons, Bradley?"

Jenny shrugged. "In my two years here, they haven't turned up on my radar".

"Well then you've been fortunate so far," Hardy replied. "The Hemon family have a long list of encounters with the law – drug charges, burglary; they had their hand in a number of rackets around the city. Jimmy Hemon, the dad, always ran the show but he's presently spending time in HMP. His sons, Charlie and Mark, are in the family business, as is Judy Hemon, their mother. It's fair to say, if there are any big scams going on, there will be a Hemon involved somewhere."

"Any obvious thoughts who would want Charlie dead?" Jenny asked.

Hardy snorted. "Where do you start? They're a hot-headed bunch and there'd be no shortage of candidates who'd like to see them disappear. Starting with members of their own family. Jimmy kept his family together by putting the fear of God in them, but there's no love between the brothers. The first person I'd go and chat to about Charlie is his older brother Mark."

Jenny passed the evidence bag across the desk.

"Does this mean anything to you? It was found on Charlie's body."

Hardy looked blankly at the playing card. "It was found on him?" He passed it back. "The Jack of Clubs. I'd say that wasn't a bad choice for Charlie Hemon. He is - or rather I should say was - a right Jack the lad."

Jenny took the card and stood, ready to leave.

"Hardy, you know the Chief far better than I do. He seems very riled by this case."

"I'm sure he is. He's not a fan of the media spotlight and when it leaks out we've been looking in Spain for a man who's been dead under a tree in Bristol for two years, it won't make us look too bright.

Plus, the Hemon family have been a thorn in his side for years. I expect he was looking forward to wiping the suntanned smile off Charlie's face."

Hardy shrugged "I can't say I'm sorry it landed in your lap, rather than mine."

Jenny looked at him in surprise. "You didn't want to be leading this one?"

"Good God, no. It will be under intense scrutiny from the press and the higher echelons of the national police. It'll be a headache I'm happy to avoid."

Jenny opened her mouth to reply, but thought better of it. She thanked him and left his office, distracted by his last comment. If Hardy wasn't pushing for the high profile work, why had the Chief chosen him over her? It made his decision even more baffling.

#

"Our best place to find Mark is at his girlfriend's place," Will said, as they turned off the main road. Will had been involved with investigations into the Hemon clan many times before. He didn't even need to add the address of the Lawrence Weston estate into the GPS.

They parked amongst the pillars of grey concrete blocks, the same colour as the heavy dark clouds above. Jenny followed behind Will's tall stature and his easy double-step stride up the stairwell to the white painted door of number forty-seven. He waited for Jenny to join him, raised an eyebrow to check she was ready, and knocked loudly.

The door was pulled open instantly.

"Hello, Donna," Will said, to the surprised expression greeting him. The tiny figure was dressed smartly, her hair pulled back tight and her lipstick freshly applied. "I guess you were expecting someone else?"

She watched him warily, not moving, but not shutting them out.

"Can we come in?"

Donna reluctantly stood to one side to let Will and Jenny into the living room. She gestured them towards the sofa, where a line of bright red cushions were evenly spaced.

"I'm DI Jenny Bradley. Sorry to disturb you, but we're looking for Mark Hemon. Is he around?"

Donna perched on the very edge of the sofa and spoke for the first time.

"Mark's not been here for ages."

"When did you last see him?" Jenny asked, watching Donna carefully. She seemed taut but resigned to dealing with the police, as if it was familiar territory to her.

"I don't know, last year sometime. He was always disappearing for a few weeks, never saying where. Then he just… never came back."

"Do you have a way to contact him?" Will asked.

"I had a number, but he never picked up. He never wanted me to phone him anyway."

Jenny smoothed her hands over her skirt before clasping them together. She drew in a deep breath and looked directly at Donna, carefully gauging her reactions.

"I'm afraid we have bad news about his brother Charlie."

Donna looked at her coldly.

"We've found his body. It looks like he was murdered."

Donna's shoulders dropped slightly. Jenny got the strong impression this news came as a relief. "You think Mark did it? Is that why you're here?"

"Do you think he would kill his own brother?" Jenny asked.

Donna's face darkened. "You clearly didn't know them." She walked over to the window and stared down at the grim street below.

Will excused himself to use the bathroom. Out of the corner of her eye, Jenny saw him slipping down the corridor, past the bathroom and into the single bedroom. Jenny kept Donna talking until she heard the toilet flush and Will returned with a slight shake of his head.

"One more thing." Jenny slid the Jack of Clubs card, still in its plastic bag, across the table. "Have you seen this before?"

Donna frowned as she picked up the card.

"Never seen it before," she said, handing it back with a shrug.

"We found it on Charlie's body."

She saw a brief flash in Donna's eyes, just the smallest of movements, before she blinked it away.

"Never seen it," she said more vehemently, and shook her head.

Jenny retrieved the playing card from the table and replaced it with a Police contact card. "If anything ever comes to mind, just ask for Will or myself," she said.

As they drove back towards town, Will reported on his brief search of the flat. A man's razor was in the bathroom cabinet, and there were a pair of shoes under the bed that were definitely not Donna's.

"But they're not Mark's either," Will concluded. "Mark's a short arse, short and mean, and those shoes were far too big. I suspect they belong to the man she was all dressed up to see this afternoon. Mark must have been gone for some time; there's no way she'd dare have another guy in her life if he was still around."

Jenny nodded. "I think she's lying about the playing card, though," she said. "There was something in her reaction. I'm sure she'd seen it before."

Only then did Jenny realise what she'd seen in Donna's eyes. It wasn't only recognition. It was fear.

#

Jenny's car joined the slow creep of morning rush-hour traffic over the suspension bridge and her mind was preoccupied with the case so far. Her phone rang, and Will's number came up.

"I think we might want to go straight to Long Grove," he said, his voice tinny over the speaker. "Something's come up on their employment records. I've checked everyone who was there around the time Charles was killed. There's one name – Sam Brently – with a Bristol address. He's got a record, a couple of burglary and assault charges, and he left Long Grove in May two years ago. I can't find any record of him since then. The address he listed, 161 Richmond Road, Montpelier, doesn't exist."

"I'll meet you there," Jenny said. "Call Mr Cooper and tell him we're on our way over. And see if his boss is back from his tropical jaunt."

She pulled out of the queue of traffic and turned into the clear roads leading away from the city.

#

In the wood panelled front room of the house, Mr Cooper twitched in his chair overlooking the grounds. He kept running his fingers through his long greying hair as Jenny and Will quizzed him on the subject of his former employee.

"I can't really remember Sam Brently," he said, biting the chapped skin around his fingers.

"Would you have been the one to interview and employ him?" Jenny asked.

"Well yes, officially, but sometimes when things are desperate, and then when someone knows someone who is free…"

"And references and background checks?" Will asked, looking up from his notebook.

Cooper's face paled further.

"It gets so busy here, and if the staff are only working in the garden, I don't always... the boss is going to be furious." He shook his head.

"We'd like to speak to him," Jenny said.

Cooper rose and nodded. "Yes, yes, he's expecting you."

As if on cue the door opened and a stocky man strode in, sports jacket buttoned tight and hair combed smooth. His face was tanned, his expression bullish.

"Detective, Sergeant, I'm Justin Roberts." Jenny shook the hand thrust towards her. "How can we get this matter sorted?"

Jenny watched carefully as Will quizzed Roberts about Sam Brently and any possible connection with the man found murdered on the grounds. Roberts' answers were brisk and businesslike, but a question of his own caught her attention.

"Do you know how long this body has been underground?" he asked. "Has it been over two years?"

"We currently believe that's the case, yes," Will said.

"Well, that puts us in the clear, I believe. We only bought that section of woodland two years ago."

Jenny looked up in surprise. "Really? Mr Cooper implied..."

"I can find you the paperwork on the sale. We bought it when our neighbour died. He'd been there for years. I'll find it for you."

Roberts left, and the sharp click of his footsteps receded down the hallway. Cooper, who had been standing by the window while his boss was talking, twisting his hands over each other, sat down with a sigh of relief.

"Why did you not mention this before, Mr Cooper?" Jenny

didn't trouble to mask her irritation. She didn't like having things concealed from her.

"I never thought he'd been underground so long. He looked so real, so new. It didn't occur to me. But now, to think this nightmare might not have happened on my watch... I can't tell you what a relief that is."

#

Back in the team's bustling office, Jenny opened the files Roberts had given her relating to the purchase of the tract of land where Charlie Hemon had been buried. The land had been part of a large neighbouring estate owned by a Mr Brian Hoday. On his death, his extended family, had decided to sell off some of the land before refurbishing the main house and the many separate outhouses.

Jenny put the address into the police records, pursing her lips as the screen revealed a file from a year before the land was sold. There was evidence that two of the old outhouses had been used for growing pot. Surely, she thought, for Charlie Hemon to turn up dead just where a local drug production had been in full flow was no coincidence.

Jenny opened the transcript of the interview with Hoday at the time of the discovery. He had been the one to find the plants and call the police and the report concluded that the plants were removed and destroyed, but no charges were ever brought against anyone.

Jenny read through the transcript again. Something was nagging at her, and she scrolled back up the page until she found what had caught her eye.

Mr Hoday had said he rarely went to the outhouses, but he had recently put the land up for sale with a local estate agent and wanted to check their condition.

It was the same estate agent who subsequently sold the land to

Justin Roberts a year later, after Hoday had died.

Jenny sent Will a link to the files and called the estate agent, arranging to meet the manager the following morning. As she put down the phone her eyes were drawn to the oak tree playing card, resting on her desk. She picked it up and studied it, turning it over in her hand. Why would anyone leave this? There was nothing special about it; it was a mass produced playing card…

An idea came into her head that made her heart freeze. She sat motionless for a moment, then picked up her phone and stepped out into the corridor. She slipped into a small meeting room opposite, where she was sure she wouldn't be overheard, and dialled her friend's number.

#

Jenny stretched out on her sofa, the meal-for-one lasagne sitting on her plate. She hadn't bothered to take it out of the tin foil; there was no one here to criticise her and it saved washing up. She placed her wine glass on the coffee table and flipped the TV over to the news. The murder had slipped off top spot, replaced by the threat of a tube strike in London. Just as her boss appeared on screen for the televised press conference, her mobile rang.

"Will, what's up? I'm watching the Chief do his thing."

"Sorry guv, just an update. I'll keep it brief. I was chatting to a couple of guys who used to hang out with Charlie and they'd heard of Brently. It doesn't sound like he's a massive player in the Hemon's schemes, but their paths certainly crossed."

"Has anyone seen Brently recently?" She stuck the fork into the lasagne.

"Not as far as I can tell. Sounds like he left town a couple of years back."

"What about Mark Hemon? Any leads on his whereabouts?"

"The general consensus is he's drinking up the Spanish sunshine with his mother. They have a house near Malaga. Everyone presumed Charlie was down there with them."

"Do we know what the man posing as Charlie was arrested for?"

"Yes, the Spanish police picked him up over a fight in a bar," Will told her. "They contacted the UK as he's a British citizen, but he was released and out on bail before his name came up on our system."

"OK. Shame we got the message too late. With this drug discovery, the police confiscated a couple of van loads of plants shortly before Charlie was killed. I'm guessing someone wasn't happy when the business was discovered. Mark is the obvious suspect, but let's check who else they might they have been working with."

Jenny had kept half an ear on Ross making his statement while she was talking to Will. Earlier in the afternoon she had told the boss they were searching for Sam Brently, but now she realised he had never mentioned his name during the press conference. She felt a flash of annoyance with her boss for disregarding a lead she considered important. What was his problem anyway?

#

Jenny switched her phone to silent and slid it back into her pocket. The estate agency was quiet when she entered. The jaunty angled desks, each with their suited occupants, made it unclear whom she should talk to. She took out her badge and flashed it at the nearest suit.

"I have a ten o'clock appointment with the manager," she said. The young man rose and led her to an office away from the front desks and the customers.

She accepted his offer of coffee. She hadn't needed to show her badge, but sometimes it was too tempting. It usually made things happen considerably faster.

An older man came over and introduced himself as Paul Greenford, the company manager. "You're interested in the land purchase over in Long Grove, is that right?" He opened a file on his desk and handed across a sheet of A4.

"This is proof of purchase of the land to Mr J Roberts. I personally dealt with this matter, but I don't remember any difficulties with the sale. Could I ask what this is in relation to?"

"The recently discovered murder victim was found in this woodland," Jenny said briskly, putting the paper down. "I read there was evidence of drugs being grown in the outhouses. Was this raised during the sale?"

The estate agent frowned. "That does ring a bell. It came up in a previous sale, I think." He turned to a filing cabinet behind him, rifled through the drawer and pulled out a folder.

"There was an attempted sale about a year before the owner died. The area was pretty much wasteland, very overgrown." He flicked through the paperwork, his eyes scanning the pages. "The potential buyer was a Susan Crosner. I seem to remember she was interested in buying the land to create an arboretum and was applying for grants, but the applications stalled when she discovered the outhouses were being used to grow marijuana – a little cottage industry out there from the sounds of things. The owner was very upset."

"I'm sorry, did you say Ms Crosner found the drug factories?"

The estate agent looked down at this notes.

"I'm pretty sure she did. I think she was the one to tell Mr Hoday. I don't think he knew anything about them before but he took the land off the market while the investigation was underway As far as I know, they never found out who was growing it – but then I guess you would know that."

Jenny returned his smile. "Did Ms Crosner show any interest in the land when it came up for sale a year later?"

The estate agent shook his head and returned his attention to the first file on the desk. 'No, I don't believe she did. Mr Roberts was the only one to make an offer."

Jenny took out her notebook. "Would you have contact details for Ms Crosner?" The estate agent clicked his computer into life and read out a mobile number.

Jenny shook his hand goodbye, and dialled Will's number as she walked back to the car.

"Morning. How was the meeting? I'm chasing a frustrating paper trail …something doesn't add up…"

"Hold that thought, I can't talk for long," Jenny interrupted, "What can you find out about a Susan Crosner? She might have been the first one to discover the drugs on the property, but she's not mentioned in the police report. Let's try and find out if she saw anything that could connect the drugs to the Hemons."

"Right, will do. Where are you heading? Are you not coming in?"

Jenny paused, choosing her words carefully. "I would," she said, "but I'm meeting an old friend. I'll be in touch soon."

#

The tiny airstrip used by gliders and amateur pilots was deserted except for a single Cessna, parked up at the end of the runway. The only visible figures were standing next to the concrete clubhouse. Jenny smiled when she recognized Dan's unruly hair and tweed jacket. He was heading towards her with a younger man at his side.

"Hello darling!" he said, arms held wide to hug her as she approached. "What, no uniform? I thought I would at least see you with all your buckles and badges."

"Hilarious as always," Jenny said with a smile. "It's good to see you. And thank you for doing this at such short notice. I hope it's not going to be a waste of your time."

"Thanks are hardly needed. I can't tell you how excited I was when you called.

Jenny, this is James, my new research student. James, this is Detective Inspector Jenny Bradley."

Dan saw Jenny's hesitation. "Don't panic, Jenny, James knows this is all very hush hush." He grinned wildly.

The three of them walked across the grass to the plane. "I had to pull in a few favours, but I've been looking for an excuse to test one of these for a while,' Dan said as he climbed on board and greeted the pilot, who was running through pre-flight checks.

"Dan, this is just a wild hunch..." Jenny said with concern.

"I know. But it's your hunch, and in my book that makes it worth following up. Come and see the camera, it's already in place."

The hyperspectral camera was positioned under the main fuselage of the plane. Wires running from the camera linked to a control panel and screen inside the cabin.

"How does it work exactly?" Jenny asked. "All I know is it can detect where earth has been disturbed."

"Essentially any subterranean activity influences the frequency of light emitted above ground," James explained, while Dan rolled his eyes. "The camera can pick up these light frequencies and can be used to detect these changes."

Dan picked up the explanation. "It's actually detecting the impact ground movements have on plant growth. If you dig up an area, it has a negative impact on the established plants and triggers new growth, and that emits a different frequency of light."

Dan paused and looked across at her. "On the phone you said an aerial survey could be very revealing. Before I jump to conclusions, can you tell me what you think could be down there?"

"I have no idea to be honest. Probably nothing at all…"

Dan watched her intently and Jenny explained her thinking.

"The body we found wasn't dumped or discarded, but carefully dug under a large oak tree. I'm sure the type of tree is significant – but exactly what it signifies I have yet to find out."

Jenny opened her bag and pulled out a map of the estate grounds. "I need to rule out the chance that there are more bodies down there. I have no real reason to suspect there are – but it would give me peace of mind. I am sorry this is unofficial, Dan, but I have a boss on my back who wants this case out of the way without any undue press excitement. A ground search of the entire area would have ruffled too many nervous feathers."

Dan fumbled in the top right-hand pocket of his jacket for his glasses and peered at the map. "If there's a lot of ground cover or a thick tree canopy, we'll struggle to get a good image of the earth. But buried bodies have a huge impact on plant growth. A fully intact body initially prohibits plant life, but as soon as decomposition kicks in, it becomes good fertiliser and the vegetation cover blooms. If there's someone buried close to the surface and we can get a clear view of the ground, we should be able to detect it. Strap in."

"No way," Jenny rose, almost bumping her head on the low ceiling of the cabin. "I'm a lousy flyer, and I'm already hiding off the work radar. I need to get back. But you will call me as soon as you get down?"

"Of course. It'll take a good few hours to analyse the images though."

"I understand. And I owe you" Jenny said, jumping the last few steps to the tarmac of the runway.

The propellers ticked into life and the plane began to accelerate.

She saw Dan waving cheerily as the Cesna took off, veering southwards towards Bristol.

\#

He cast his eyes along the rose bushes edging the garden path; the neat lines of thorny stems stood mutely to attention like a well-behaved class. He eased the black glove onto his right hand and picked up the gardening shears from the hook by the back door. His steady morning walk up the ranks left dark, evenly spaced steps in the dew. Occasionally he stepped out of line to pause and snip off any small aberration.

His daily rounds helped him to think, to plan, to ponder his options. Charlie's premature discovery was a considerable frustration but, as he reminded himself, the best laid plans oft go astray.

The playing card had never been mentioned in the police press reports. Maybe it would have been better if it was? If it had, his latest delivery would have injected a fear in the recipient's heart that would have been very satisfying to observe.

Yet he knew his next target would disappear at even the slightest whiff of trouble. He might miss his chance to finish what he had started. Inflicting terror alone would not be enough. It would never give him the satisfaction he craved.

He prised a snail from the garden wall behind the rose bed and threw it on to the patio in front of him. He watched carefully as the snail's antennae gradually emerged to test for danger before it began to slide back to the wall. He eased his foot down, enjoying the satisfying crunch as its shell caved in under the sole of his boot.

\#

When Jenny arrived at the station, Will was nervously pacing the smoker's corner of the car park. "Are you ok?" she asked, accepting the cigarette he held out to her.

"No, I'm not. There's total confusion in Spain. I've been trying to find out when we might get to interview the man arrested as Charlie Hemon, but the Malaga branch who first arrested him... well they aren't even looking for him. They had no idea he was wanted in connection with a murder. Also, no one in the station knows anything about the Hemon extradition."

Will slid his hands over his face in exasperation. "We're in danger of letting this impostor slip away."

"But the Chief is in contact with the head of the Spanish investigation, isn't he? What has he said about it?"

"He's in meetings in London all day today. No one can get hold of him. The extradition order is in our files with Hardy's signature on it, but there's no clear paper chain after that. My guess is, the order is still in with the head of the Spanish PD and due to some mighty cock up, it hasn't been sent through to the local department."

"Christ," said Jenny. The cigarette trembled in her fingers as she took a drag. "Have we got anything from the Spanish? Anything to help ID who's over there?"

"Nothing. No photos, no descriptions. I'll send them Mark Hemon's mugshot and see if anyone recognizes him."

"Any leads on Sam Brently?"

"Nothing so far. I'll keep digging. Oh, and I've arranged an appointment to see Jimmy Hemon at HMP Bristol, to see if the old man knows what his sons were up to."

"Great. I'd like to meet him, especially after hearing so much about the elusive Hemon clan," said Jenny.

"I wouldn't get too excited. He's not usually very talkative," Will said, squashing the end of his cigarette into the bin. "But I did find Susan Crosner's mother and left a message for her to call. The mobile number you gave me for Susan was cut off."

Jenny nodded

"So how was your old friend?"

Her reply was stalled by the ring tone of her phone in her bag. To her surprise, Dan's name was flashing on the screen. "Speak of the devil. I need to take this." She turned and walked away from Will to a quiet corner of the car park.

"Dan, that was quick. I'm presuming it was a waste of time?"

Dan's voice was rushed and excited and it instantly filled her with dread. "On the contrary, there are definitely signs of disturbances – no shortage of animal dens, probably badgers and rabbits – but there are areas that don't fit the normal wildlife profiles. We would need to do a visual check on the ground for any animal activity before I could be certain."

Jenny changed direction and headed towards her car, ignoring Will's shout. "Can you get to the estate before dark? I'm leaving town now, I'll meet you there."

#

As the weak spring light faded into grey dusk, the outline of the Long Grove mansion once again appeared in Jenny's field of view. Instead of neatly sorting out the death of a local thug, as her boss had hoped, she feared she was about to open a huge can of worms. She knew she should call the Chief, but she found herself stalling. This was her case, and she wanted to be sure she wasn't about to make a huge fool of herself.

The press had left their round-the-clock vigil in the car park and Jenny was relieved there would be few prying eyes around. If the images from the hyperspectral camera were no more than underground fox dens, she wanted to find out as quickly and quietly as possible.

Jenny parked away from the entrance to the building to avoid meeting either Cooper or Roberts. She checked her watch, and was about to call Dan and ask him where the hell he was when she spotted headlights approaching down the drive. There was only about an hour of daylight left. She fervently hoped it would be enough.

Dan had the potential burial sites in his handheld GPS and they hastened up into the woodland area he had marked on a map. Occasionally he paused to fine tune their route, taking them into thick tangles of bramble that kept catching around Jenny's ankles in the approaching gloom.

"We're close. It should be near here," Dan said, waiting for the GPS screen to update. "I think about thirty metres to our right." Jenny looked up in the direction he was indicating, towards the base of a large beech tree.

The ground was covered with old leaves and small branches broken by the storm force winds. Jenny flicked on her torch and paced slowly around the tree, under the outmost span of the canopy, swiping the earth clear with her foot as she went. Nothing there. She widened her search, looking for signs of animal disturbances, but she saw nothing unusual. The ground was flat and solid, with no tunnels or den entrances. She watched Dan search the other side of the tree, shining his light under the bushes before looking at her with a shake of his head.

She looked up at the tree and the woodland around them. Surely, she thought, there were easier places to bury a body? The beech was even further into the wood than the oak; to carry a body so far from any roads would be no easy task.

"The other location is down in the valley, south of here," Dan said. 'It's hard to say for certain, but I don't think they were dug at the same time."

"What makes you think that?'

"There's a reduction in the level of blue-green light when vegetation is disturbed due to a drop in plant productivity. The next site produces a stronger reading than under this tree, which would signify the underground disturbance there is older than this one."

"So, if these are grave sites, then whoever is responsible keeps returning to dispose of his – or her – victims?"

"That would be my deduction." Dan peered intently at the map, apparently cheerfully unaffected by the possibility that they were walking in increasing darkness through a wood which might be frequently visited by a murderer.

Jenny followed him down the slope to a deep glen that was even more secluded than the beech tree. Dan stopped abruptly, his face lit by the green glow from the GPS in his hand.

"There" he said.

The branches silhouetted against the dusk sky belonged to another mighty tree. She kicked at the ground until she found something she recognized: the dried brown keys of the previous years' seeds.

"Sycamore."

She knew there was still a chance they were standing over nothing more than rabbit burrows and foxholes. If she started digging up the woodland and found nothing, she risked seriously jeopardising both the investigation and her reputation with the Chief. The press would be all over them like flies. She had little more than a hunch to justify creating such a stir.

She turned to Dan.

"Right," she said. "I'll get the team in. We'll start here."

#

When Jenny pulled into the station that evening the lights were still on in Ross' office on the first floor. She saw him move towards the window and stand looking out into the darkness, before turning back. It looked like he was either waiting for someone to arrive, or pacing back and forth across the room. Either way, she feared it might be connected to her and her exploits of the afternoon.

In the main office, Will was amongst the few still working. He looked up with some curiosity as she walked in, and was about to speak when she held her hand up and gestured towards the boss' room.

She walked up the stairs and knocked sharply, opening the door before she heard his answer.

"Sir, I've instructed the scene of crime team to investigate two more areas in the woodland vicinity."

He leant against his desk. She waited for him to speak, but he just looked at her in silence.

"I want to rule out the possibility of finding any other bodies in the area. Analysis with a hyperspectral camera that can detect underground disturbances located two coordinates that could be potential gravesites. The team will continue to use ground penetrating radar in the morning to assess the locations before any potential excavations."

The Chief started to prowl the office once more. "What makes you think there are more bodies out there?" he asked.

Jenny swallowed hard. "It's the card, sir, the oak tree card on the body. It looks like it was there to be discovered – like a signature, from whoever put him underground. It was deliberately done and that got me thinking. The card comes from a set. I suspect the same might be true of the body."

She was suddenly struck by how old the Chief looked. The bright overhead light cast shadows across his haggard face.

"Sir, I'm sorry I didn't clear this with you but I…"

"Have they found anything yet?" Ross cut in.

"No sir. They'll continue at first light."

The Chief's face softened for the first time.

"We'll wait and see before we announce anything to the press. I agree with your hunch here, Bradley. I'm impressed."

She felt herself flush at the unexpected praise. "Thank you, sir. Thank you."

Will was alone in the office when she returned. She pulled out the seat next to him and sat down with a huge sigh of relief.

"Will, I'm sorry I've been keeping you in the dark."

He shrugged. "I'm guessing the boss approved of whatever you've been up to?"

"It was a far better reaction than I expected, I must say. How about we catch up over a pint? My round?"

Will's eyebrows shot up in surprise and he instantly turned his computer off. "Sounds good to me."

As they crossed the car park towards the Bay Horse, Jenny looked back towards the Chief's office. His light was still on and she was sure she had just seen him back away from the window and that he was once again pacing the room, but the barrage of Will's questions about exactly what she had been up to soon distracted her. If Ross wanted to prowl around his office, she wasn't going to let it worry her. She was just glad he hadn't bitten her head off for going after her hunch. She would, she was sure, soon have this case in the bag.

#

"This police invasion was supposed to be over. Our estate is tainted forever by all the negative press coverage – and now this!" Justin Robert's hand jerked theatrically at the line of vans parked in the driveway of his Long Grove estate.

Jenny groaned inwardly. Six am was too early to deal with Roberts and his irate blustering. She was cold, and she was under-caffeinated. "Mr Roberts, I appreciate your concern, but I'm afraid you have to let the investigation follow all lines of enquiry." She stamped her feet to keep her blood moving in the frosty morning air.

"But what the hell is going on? Do you even have the right to come barging in like this? Do you know how many wedding bookings we've lost already?"

"Mr Roberts, until we find out what happened, we must investigate all lines of enquiry," Jenny repeated, mustering a display of patience she was far from feeling. "I appreciate this is an unsavoury time of day for all concerned. I will ensure you are kept informed of any developments." She turned away and followed the procession, her mist-fuelled breath preceding her up the hillside.

Dan was in the middle of a huddle, leaning over a table scattered with images from the hyperspectral camera. He was enthusiastically explaining the intricacies of the camera detection system to the men and women around him. Jenny was struck by how excited he was that the technology might have helped them to hit gold. He was unconcerned about the macabre nature of the treasure they sought. It was almost a game to him.

The sycamore was by far the most impressive tree in the valley, with thick branches radiating in all directions from the vast trunk. Its spring buds were just starting to break, and within weeks the dense network of leaves would obscure the sky, but in this early March morning, light could still reach the forest floor. Jenny watched as the team, lit by the cool grey dawn, methodically wheeled the ground penetrating radar over the base of the great tree, the operator watching a screen to see a grainy image of what lay underneath.

There was nothing Jenny could do but wait to see what the team might find, but still she itched with frustration. She snatched at her phone as it rang, grateful to have something to do. "Will?"

"Morning to you too. Anything yet?"

"No, not so far, nothing."

"I've just had a strange phone call from Donna. She sounded upset but she didn't want to speak on the phone. I'm heading there now before our appointment with Jimmy."

"Is Mark back?"

"No idea. I'll call you as soon as I know anything. Oh, and the boss is heading your way."

"OK, thanks for the warning." The radar team had stopped a few metres from the base of the trunk and Dan was amongst the group looking intently at the screen.

"Everything ok?" asked Will.

"Yes, but I've got to go. It looks like we might have something. I'll meet you at the prison at eleven."

#

In an area around the base of the tree, the first half metre of earth had been removed and a fragment of faded red fabric was exposed to the cool spring breeze. One of the forensics officers was slowly brushing away the soil to reveal a small white button, and then the cuff of the sleeve. Jenny watched as the small wrist and long fingers of a woman's hand were exposed to the morning light.

"Oh Christ."

She turned to see who had spoken, and found Chief Superintendent Ross standing beside her. His head shook slowly, and his face was stony and resigned.

"Well Bradley, your hunch was right."

Jenny looked at the unveiled corpse. "Yes sir, it appears it was."

He stood in silence, grimacing as the hand was revealed in its shallow grave.

Jenny's phone rang. She pulled it from her pocket, expecting to see Will's name on the screen, but she didn't recognize the number that flashed up. She stepped away from the dig site and answered the call.

"Is that Detective Bradley? My name is Catherine Crosner. I was asked to call about my daughter, Susan."

It was over thirty minutes later when Jenny returned to the group, her mind racing. She found Ross still staring grimly at the excavation.

"Sir, the second team will begin work on the other location this afternoon."

He nodded, his eyes never veering away from the grave.

"I'll be back later."

"You're off to interview Jimmy Hemon? Will told me this morning. Best of luck getting anything useful out of him." It seemed despite her victories he still doubted her ability.

Jenny bit her tongue. She walked as steadily as she could out of the valley, counting her steps to keep calm until she was sure she was out of sight of the team. Only then did she lean over with her hands on her knees, forcing herself to breathe deeply.

A sound in the forest behind her made her jump. She increased her pace, not waiting to discover what had made the noise. She entered the edge of the clearing and when she could finally see the main house and the line of police cars parked alongside, she broke into a run.

#

As Jenny stepped out of the airport towards the line of hire cars she felt the warm breeze of the Spanish evening against her face. She looked at her phone, still turned off from the flight, and considered whether she should switch it back on. She knew she was keeping Will in the dark once again, but she dropped it back into her bag and drove out of the airport.

She flicked through the list of addresses she had written down from the work files. The address given to the Spanish police by the Charlie Hemon imposter would be her first stop.

An hour later, she came to a stop outside a white two-storey villa. Impressive pillars supported an ornate balcony overlooking the front garden, and around the main door a cluster of large terracotta pots sported small olive trees. She turned off her headlights and watched the house for movement. There were no lights on and the curtains were drawn on the ground floor.

She stepped out onto the deserted road and walked up the grassy edge of the pebbled driveway. She continued round to the back of the house to a garden where a swimming pool was enclosed under a thick blue cover. Everything looked undisturbed. In the corner of the patio she lifted up a tarpaulin but only found a gas fired BBQ and a garden table and chairs packed neatly away. She tried the handle on the patio door, unsurprised to find it firmly locked. This had all the hallmarks of a holiday villa packed up for the winter season, one that hadn't been lived in for weeks.

She drove to the next address on her list – the bar where the Charlie Hemon imposter had been arrested. Jenny pushed through the crowds of expats who were transfixed by a football match on the big screen at the far end of the room. The barman was stacking clean glasses on the shelves and preparing for the inevitable half time rush when Jenny caught his eye. He greeted her with a broad southern Irish accent and Jenny was relieved her rusty Spanish would not be called for.

She ordered a glass of wine and laid a photo of Mark Hemon on the bar. "I'm looking for this man, does he looked familiar to you? He could have been involved in a fight in this bar back in February, which led to an arrest."

The barman took the photo and brought it under the spot lights behind the serving hatch for a better look. He shook his head. "Sorry, no, I don't recognize him." He handed the photo back. "There was only one fight that brought the police in and I was here that night. I'm sure it wasn't him."

Jenny pulled out a photo of Sam Brently. "Was he involved? Have you seen him in here?"

The barman's face lit up. "Yeah, sure, that was him."

"Is he a regular? When did you see him last?"

"It's been a few weeks since he's shown his face round here. In fact I don't think he's been back since the fight."

Jenny nodded and slid the photo back into her folder. She pulled out one more picture and passed it over.

"Has this man also been here?"

Jenny felt her heart pulsing, the blood hot in her face. She picked up her wine in an effort to appear relaxed.

Once again, the barman took the photo under the spot to get a closer look.

"Yes, I think he might have been. He was here with your other chap, the one in the fight. He's quite a British gent so he stood out from the normal crowd we get." He gestured to the football audience with a grin.

"Thanks for your help." Jenny returned the photo to the folder with the others. As the barman was called away she slipped back out into the Spanish evening, leaving her glass of wine untouched.

#

It wasn't until half past ten the following morning when Jenny, back on British soil, finally switched on her phone. All the messages on her answer phone were from Will. The first excitedly recounted his meeting with Donna. She had seen one of these playing cards around when Mark was staying in the flat and, as Jenny had suspected, she was afraid of what they could mean. Now she was sure that Mark was back.

Will didn't elaborate on why she would have thought that, and his following messages were from outside the prison, his voice increasingly curt as he waited for her to arrive.

Jenny skipped through these until she reached his call from after his visit with Jimmy Hemon. She listened to his message once then pressed repeat to make sure she had heard it accurately. *I've just had a strange meeting with Jimmy – he's been sent one of these bloody cards – it's the Ace of Clubs with a willow tree on it. He had no idea what it was about – and for once I believe he's telling the truth. It was sent to him with no note, nothing. Donna's sure it means Mark is back…but no sign of him as yet. Oh and he knows Susan Crosner – he referred to her as 'that nosey bitch' and said they can't be linked to her car crash. I couldn't get any more from him after that. I'm looking into this car crash thing…but call me…where have you gone?*

She was about to turn the phone off again when it rang.

"Hi Will." She felt the slightest hint of guilt about the half-dozen skipped messages.

"Christ, where have you been? I've been going crazy and so has the Chief. I thought something must have happened to you!"

"Look, I'm sorry, I had to check something and I had to do it on the quiet and…"

"But you can tell me, surely? I mean, what is it with you doing everything alone?"

"Will, I'm fine. I got your messages about Jimmy and the Ace of Clubs."

"That's nothing. I'm at Long Grove and you need to get back here. The team have pulled up another body – from the other location..."

"Under the beech tree?"

"I think so... it's a damn big tree, whatever it is. I've just seen the body and we don't have formal ID yet, but I'd swear they've pulled up Mark Hemon."

Jenny froze. "Are you sure? It's definitely Mark?"

"I'd put money on it. The Chief is here and he agrees. The scene of crime team don't think he's been underground as long as Charlie, as his body is in better shape, which would fit with the last time Mark was seen around Bristol."

"Will, I need you to do two things for me. Firstly, cover for me just for today. I need a few more hours. Tell the Chief something, anything, to keep him off my back. "

Will spluttered in exasperation. "What? Where are you going now?"

"Will, please, a few more hours and then I'll need your help. There's something I have to check at the office. I'll call as soon as I can." Jenny cut the call and turned the phone off.

She put the postcode for Catherine Crosner's home address into her GPS and started the car.

#

Later that evening, Jenny turned into a quiet cul-de-sac in Sneyd Park and parked across the road from Chief Superintendent Ross' house.

She was suddenly aware of how badly her body ached with exhaustion. Her breath misted up the windscreen as she sat in the dark, preparing herself for what she knew she had to do.

Her mind ran over the phone call she had received from the coroner only a few hours earlier. He had just begun the autopsy of the two bodies discovered in the wood but he had already found an important clue. On each body, a playing card was tucked under the victims' clothes; the King of Clubs with the picture of a beech tree was on Mark Hemon's chest, and the Queen of Clubs with a sycamore was found on the female corpse.

The dead woman was yet to be formally identified, but Jenny was sure she knew who she was.

She wiped the condensation from the window and looked across at the detached brick house with its gravelled driveway. A light appeared in Ross' kitchen window and she watched as he poured himself a drink, and stood swirling the glass in his hand.

Her feet crunched on the stones and he looked up when a security light blinked into action, illuminating her entrance. She waited by the front door until the locks slid back and it finally opened.

"Inspector Bradley. This is a surprise."

She expected him to be angry, but his voice was measured and calm.

"I'm sorry to call so late, sir. Can I come in?"

He stood back to let her pass without saying a word. As she stepped into the dark wooden hallway, she was struck by the strong smell of whisky on his breath.

"Drink?" he said, rattling the ice cubes in his glass.

"Thank you sir, but I'm fine."

Jenny followed him into a sitting room where a fire was lit in the stone hearth. Ross sunk down into a sofa opposite the hearth and gestured to her to sit on the chair closest to the fire.

She felt him watching her, waiting for her to begin.

"Sir, I must apologise for being out of contact. I had good reason for it."

He nodded, placed his drink on the low glass table by his side, and leaned back with his hands clasped in his lap.

"I would hope so, Bradley. I'm looking forward to hearing what you've unearthed – so to speak." He smiled, apparently amused by his own choice of words.

"It appears Mark Hemon is now a victim, rather than a murder suspect," she began.

"Formal identification is yet to arrive, but yes, it certainly looks like him. Both Hemon brothers together," the Chief said slowly. "Who would have thought it?"

"My suspicion is the unidentified woman is Mrs Hemon, sir."

"You think so?"

"Yes, sir. I believe Charlie, Mark and his mother were killed by the same person. All three were found with a playing card featuring the type of tree they were buried under. I believe that's the murderer's calling card."

Ross nodded. "That would make sense, yes."

"But sir," Jenny said calmly, "I don't think he's finished yet."

Ross sat forward in his seat, frowning. "Go on," he said, reaching once more for the tumbler of whiskey. "What makes you think that?"

"Jimmy Hemon has received one of the killer's calling cards. He was sent the Ace of Clubs."

Ross lifted his glass to his lips and drained it dry. He sat back, nursing the empty glass in his lap. "Do you know who would be trying to eliminate all the Hemon family?"

"I think I do, sir. I'm sure Sam Brently is involved. We know he's been in Spain and I suspect he was the person posing as Charlie Hemon. I don't think Sam would have ever risked using Charlie's ID unless he knew the Hemon brothers were dead."

Ross nodded in agreement and Jenny continued.

"But I don't think he's the one sending the cards. There's someone else involved in this. Someone with a reason to bury the Hemons in this particular part of the wood."

Jenny stood up and walked across the room to the patio doors that looked out onto the immaculate garden. The external lights along the wall illuminated the perfectly straight rows of rose bushes framing either side of the lawn. She kept a close eye on her boss' reflection in the window as she spoke.

"I have just been to see Catherine Crosner. I had some questions about the death of her daughter. It turns out Susan Crosner was killed in a car crash near the woods."

Jenny turned to face her boss.

"But then you'd know all about that, wouldn't you, sir?"

Ross' expression of concern was replaced with surprise, bordering on amusement.

"Catherine Crosner told me Susan had seen who was growing drugs in the outbuildings," Jenny went on. "My guess is she saw one of the Hemons. Susan would have been a vital witness in any case against them. But one night, after leaving the estate, her car skidded off the road and she was killed."

Ross continued to watch Jenny, a smile twitching at the corner of his lips.

"I wondered why we hadn't heard about Susan's death during our investigation. But Catherine cleared that one up for me. Susan Crosner hadn't been known as Susan Crosner for long, had she? When did she start using her mother's maiden name?"

Jenny watched the smile fade from David Ross' face, but he said nothing in reply. His fingers tightened almost imperceptibly around the whiskey tumbler.

"At the time of the crash she was legally registered with her father's surname. Ross. Susan Ross. Your daughter."

Jenny saw the pain in his eyes as he pushed to his feet and walked to a drinks cabinet in the corner of the room. He picked up an unopened bottle of whiskey, twisted off the screw cap and refilled his glass.

"Are you sure you won't have one, Bradley?"

Jenny didn't answer, but waited for him to bring his glass back to the table and sit heavily back down onto the sofa.

"You suspected the Hemons were responsible for your daughter's death, that they caused her car to skid off the road that night. But there was no way you could ever prove that. I don't think you could simply let them get away..."

The Chief regarded Jenny over the top of his glass, and the smile returned to his lips.

"Is this really the theory you've been working on, Bradley? That the demise of the Hemon family is my doing? Yes, Susan was my daughter, but we hadn't spoken since she was a teenager. I had no idea she was thinking of buying land in Bristol. Dear god, Bradley, is that the best you can come up with?"

"Sir, you seem to forget I've been talking to Catherine," Jenny pressed on, undeterred. "She told me how devastated you were when Susan was killed. How much you regretted not speaking to your daughter for years. I expect you were upset that she had finally changed her surname, although that did mean no one realised who her father was."

Ross shook his head in disbelief. "I knew I should have put Hardy on this case. I must apologise for not letting you know about my daughter, but it was personal matter, not one I ever thought would become important to this case..."

"I know you were in Spain," Jenny interrupted. "You were with Sam Brently shortly before the discovery of Charlie's body. You prevented the extradition order for the Charlie Hemon imposter from ever reaching the Spanish police. I had Will check with the Spanish side today and they confirmed they never received the request."

Ross eyed Jenny with curiosity. "You've certainly been busy, I'll give you that. It's just a shame you've poured all your energies into such a ludicrous theory. Tell me Bradley, exactly what impact do you think it will have on your career to put such wild accusations on the record? Have you thought what a fool you will look? That you will always be known as the officer who accused their superior of …well what is it now….triple murder and manipulating police paperwork?"

Ross stood up and walked over to Jenny. "You'll never progress up the ladder with such a stain on your record. It's career suicide, Bradley. Take my advice and let this one drop. This Brently chap sounds like your man. From what you've uncovered, it seems he's been living happily off Charlie Hemon's cash in Spain, which sounds like motive enough to me."

Jenny opened her mouth to speak, but Ross edged closer to her and continued. "I'll give you credit where credit is due though, Bradley. You have strong instincts and the conviction to pursue them. That's a very valuable quality, something that we need in every DCI in the force. There is a new position coming up soon and I can ensure your name is at the top of the list."

Jenny was aware the Chief was gripping her arm tightly. A banging on the door startled them both. The blue flashing light of a police car illuminated the hallway behind them.

"Did you really think you'd need back up, Bradley?" The Chief let go of her and walked over to open the front door. Will and three uniformed officers stood on the step.

"Evening, boys," he said, as if nothing unusual was taking place. "Wait here one moment, please?" He closed the door again, and returned to where Jenny was standing.

"It's not too late to call the dogs off, Bradley. I'd advise you to do just that before you make the worst mistake of your life. "

Jenny looked at her boss, his body suddenly taut, strained, his face flushed with whisky and heat.

"You know what's been puzzling me? Why you'd do any of this. I thought maybe it was your frustration with the Hemons. You've been trying to stop their schemes for years, but somehow they always managed to slip away. They kept beating the system – and now you suspected they were getting away with murder. It offended your sense of order. But now, I think it was more basic than that. If your daughter had told you who she'd seen in the outhouses, you would have known she was in danger. But she didn't. You admit you didn't know she was buying land in Bristol. You had cut her out of your life so completely she even stopped using your name. But if you had been there for her, if she had been able to turn to you for help, she might still be alive. You failed her as a father, and you know it."

Ross stood motionless. "So thank you sir, for the advice and your offer, but I won't be calling the dogs off." Jenny walked past him, opened the door and gestured for Will and the officers to come in.

When no one moved, Jenny instructed two of the uniforms to escort Chief Superintendent Ross to the station. He did nothing to resist being led to the waiting car, but as he ducked into the back seat, he called Jenny over and said something in her ear that only she would hear.

#

Will and Jenny were left on the Chief's front lawn as the car taking their boss to the station disappeared from view.

Will was the first to break the silence. "Christ. What happened in there?"

Jenny shook her head. "He didn't admit to killing the Hemons. But he will."

Will stared at her. Jenny pulled her coat tightly round her and fumbled in the pocket for her cigarettes.

"I have yet to find anyone who knew the Chief had a daughter. Even Hardy didn't know."

Jenny regarded Will with surprise.

"You've spoken to Hardy? What was his reaction?"

"He thinks you're stark raving mad to suspect the Chief. I seriously thought he was about to have another hernia when I told him what was going on."

Jenny smiled. "I expect that's why Ross wanted Hardy to lead the team. He knows Hardy would never suspect him."

"But there's more I don't understand," Will said. "Why would he get involved with Sam Brently?"

"While Sam was posing as Charlie Hemon, no one realised Charlie was missing. I'm sure Mark Hemon and his mother thought Charlie was in Spain, and that was exactly what the Chief needed. He didn't want any of them to suspect they had become a target and risk them disappearing from Bristol. Meanwhile, Sam had access to Charlie's bank account and was happily living it up on the Spanish coast."

"The Chief must have been getting money to Brently. I'll look into his accounts," Will said.

Jenny nodded. "If we find Sam, we can ask him. But I doubt we will. I imagine he outlived his usefulness as soon as Charlie's body was discovered."

"Bloody hell. Do you think…?"

"Yes I do. I expect Brently was involved in the drug growing operation too. In the Chief's mind, he was also linked to his daughter's death."

Will slowly paced around the Chief's gravel drive, his boots crunching on the loose stones. "But what about the playing cards?"

"Catherine Crosner helped answer that one. The cards used to belong to Susan," Jenny said. "She told me when Susan was young, she would spend hours gardening with her dad. She shared the Chief's passion for plants. He bought her the cards to help identify the trees when they were walking in the woods. When she was killed, it was the one thing of hers he asked to keep."

"Still," Will shuddered, "why leave them on the bodies? It's symbolic, but it's a bit weird…"

"I've been puzzling over that one too. I'm convinced the Chief couldn't cope with the guilt of his daughter's death. They hadn't spoken since she was a teenager, but when she died, he discovered she was trying to buy a woodland. She wanted to build an arboretum, and she was killed following a passion that came from her afternoon walks with her dad… It kind of fits. Did you get a chance to check the Chief's schedule?"

"Yes," Will said. "As you suggested, I went back through his diary and made a note of when he booked time off. There are three occasions that could coincide with the times the bodies were buried. On each occasion he had the time booked off as gardening leave."

"Gardening leave. Christ." Jenny shook her head in disbelief. "The clues were all there for us to find. Do you recall when we first identified Charlie's body, he asked why Charlie was fertilising an oak tree? I didn't think anything of it at the time, but it was a strange comment. Why not just ask why he was dead and buried? Who would instantly think of a body as fertiliser? But that's what the Hemons had become to him. The playing cards were there to pay his twisted respects to his daughter – while each tree would be fed by the people he blamed for her death."

Jenny looked back at her boss's impeccably tidy house.

"I think he could justify what he was doing to himself, but deep down, at some level, he knew it was wrong. Fundamentally, it went against what he stood for, what he had believed in all his working life. I think that's why he left the clues. Maybe at some level he wanted to see if the police could solve it. He wanted to test if the proper order of things could be restored."

Will let out a long, slow sigh. "Are you confident he'll admit to it?"

"Yes, yes he will now," Jenny said "Do you know what he said to me just before he was driven away tonight?"

Will shook his head.

"He said, 'nice work, Bradley, nicely done.'"

FISHER OF MEN

By Justin Newland

"*C*apitan, the tide is full, when can we sail?" John Cabot asked me, his thick accent betraying his Venetian origins.

"We're ready, Master, save two additions to the crew."

"Just so," he replied. He motioned to the quay where a crowd had gathered, excited by the departure of the Matthew and driven by any opportunity to find food in these days of scarcity. They parted like the Red Sea when a man in a black cloak and white habit passed amongst them. Behind him limped another man, his lay assistant, I assumed. The Black Friar strode up the gangplank, followed by a line of porters each carrying a large bundle of twigs on their backs.

As he boarded the ship, from beneath the drapes of his cassock he pulled a rough-hewn crucifix which he held up to the heavens. He mumbled some blessed thing and brushed past my shoulder.

"Wait! What madness is this?" I asked. "These men bring tinder on board. One spark and we'll all be sent to heaven." I stepped in front of the first man in line. The stench of ale on his breath was rank. His mouth displayed teeth as rotten as the Holy Roman Church.

The Black Friar lowered his hood, revealing dim eyes, gaunt cheeks and a face as wrinkled as a dried fig.

"Whoever you are, how dare you impede the work of the Almighty?" He glared at me with eyes of liquid fire. "Show these men to the hold."

"I will not! The hold is already full – with victuals for the long journey."

"By the Lord our Christ, I am a fisher of men. Remove them,

make room for the fasces. These bundles of twigs are essential to the success of this holy expedition." He spat the words out like poisoned morsels of food.

I was about to question him further when I felt a dig in my ribs. It was John Cabot. He whispered in my ear.

"The Friar bears the Seal of the Holy Office of the Inquisition."

I knew resistance was futile. He was a Dominican, the order of mendicant friars who sustained themselves through alms alone. They occupied a curious nether-world, suspended between heaven and earth, where their infamous austerity and absolute insistence of religious purity made them incorrigible representatives of the Pope in all matters of the Inquisition.

While the crew dumped precious food and water onto the quay, the crowd erupted into a riot of screams and fighting. They ravaged the discarded supplies, men fighting over a loaf, women scratching each other, and children stealing what morsels they could. In all my years at the helm, I'd never sailed with such a cargo, but this was no ordinary voyage. John Cabot had read to me from the letters patent from none other than King Henry VII himself, '*Free authority to sail to all parts under our banners, there to find countries of heathens, in whatsoever part of the world placed, which before this time were unknown to all Christians*.'

Once the fasces were loaded, I spied the Black Friar's lay assistant on the quay as he concealed a stray loaf in his tunic. He sloped up the gangplank carrying a cage covered with a black cloth. I assumed it to be a bird cage.

"S-sorry about your supplies." His voice was soft as the waters of the Avon.

"We will all be." I sighed. "What do they call you?"

"G-g-g-geb Drum." He had a neck like a goose, a crook nose and sleepy eyes that blinked as if he was walking through a hailstorm.

"Look after that loaf of bread," I suggested with a wink.

"I w-will," he stammered and went on his way.

Before weighing anchor, the Friar spoilt us with an impromptu sermon. "It is our religious duty to discover the new land, and there welcome every lost savage into the arms of Christendom." His words brought the fires of the inquisition right into Bristow dock. From the terrified look on Geb's face, I knew I was not alone in abhorring the righteous Dominican.

I was glad to leave the markets and alleys of Bristow behind. There as a young man, I'd stolen a loaf of bread for my starving children from the monks. For my sins, I'd been confined to the stocks, spat upon and humiliated, shackled by a suffocating religion. My wife and children died of the plague so I too was driven to sea. Now I needed to find the virgin land.

The sway and pitch of the ship's movement soon made me forget the Friar. I looked forward to the routine of life at sea and my two watches – dawn and dusk. The next day, Geb emerged onto deck as the first slither of dawn bled out of the sky. His shadow huddled over the cage beneath the mast. As he lifted off the black cloth, inside the cage were two snow white doves. At dusk he returned. And every day thereafter, he'd come and feed the cooing pair with morsels of his loaf.

Ten days into the Atlantic and I sat whittling a piece of wood, lost in the ocean's vast, audacious beauty. To my surprise, Geb opened the cage and released the doves. They fluttered around the ship, once, twice, thrice, before one settled on the rigging, the other on the main mast, preening themselves. In the gathering gloom, they looked like shimmering white angels, full of the spirit of the Holy Ghost.

#

During those days of squall and swell, as the winds howled and the rains lashed the deck, we squeezed into our quarters. The crew murmured that sooner or later the Matthew would reach the edge of the world and topple into the fires of Hell. I was convinced the Dominican was stoking the men's superstitions with whispers of doom. That was the way he kept them held in the palm of his hand. The crew could take succour from him; that was their choice. I preferred to listen to the creak and groan of the ships' timbers as she rose and fell to the wild tune of the ocean, safe in the knowledge that she was hewn from solid English oak. That was my solace.

We'd been at sea the days numbered by the temptation of Christ in the wilderness, or so the Friar delighted in reminding us. Pulled north by north east by a vital current, we followed huge shoals of brown-backed fish as long as my arm. They were tantalisingly close, yet we'd no means to fish them. Beneath his black hood, I was sure those lips wore a demonic smile, delighting in our misfortune. Why? Our supplies had dwindled to crumbs and shreds. No-one could eat tinder. Where was his Christian charity?

At dawn, when Geb unlatched the cage, the birds refused to fly into the mists, preferring to stay on their perches with their heads tucked into their chests. Later that day, the Friar celebrated mass. "The morrow brings us the glory of the Feast of St. John the Baptist," he cried, drops of water dripping from his hood. Like Geb, we bent the knee and pressed our palms together.

The Friar chastised us. "God Almighty has punished us with this blinding fog. All because you're sinners!"

In truth, the men feared the edge of the world more than the Black Friar and his jealous God.

Through the night and the following day, we flowed with the

currents and the legions of fish, the crew expecting at any moment to fall into the fires of perdition. At dusk a breeze blew in, and the mists began to disperse. When Geb opened the cage, both of the doves emerged, two flashes of white satin. They flew directly over the deck and out across the waters into the thinning fog. Geb reached out an arm. His face was crestfallen to see his birds disappear for the last time. John Cabot led the crew in a cheer filled with relief and thanks in equal measure. Weak from starvation, fearful of the world's edge, strangled by religious tyranny, still we were exhilarated by the discovery of a new world. The doves had taken wing; it couldn't be far.

Men are rendered by the passion of the moments they engage with, and this was one that forever after shaped our lives. From behind me came a blood-curdling cry. It was the bosun carrying a hamper. He threw it down with repugnance, spilling its contents. Legs of mutton, cartons of eggs, loaves of bread, bunches of carrots, bags of apples, jugs of water, even bottles of fine wine rolled forlornly around the deck.

"Look at all these alms I found... in the Friar's quarters," he spat.

We were of one mind.

Geb knocked him to the deck, and yelled, "Grab him!"

Holding one limb each, we lifted the Friar and swung him back and forth. He yelled and kicked. He protested his innocence. But we were empty of food as well as compassion. We threw him overboard to join his beloved fishes. When Geb told us the Friar intended to purify the heathen souls of any savage who refused to convert, we joyfully emptied the hold of his bundles of twigs.

As the mists cleared and dusk settled, another raucous cheer arose. I could just discern the silhouette of a strange new-found land.

THE TOP OF THE HILL

By Clare Dornan

"This has to be the worst plan ever."

I'm shocked to hear you say it. The distant drumming is getting louder, the raindrops hitting the forest leaves as the storm front moves in.

"We need to hurry," I say, and we both know there is no turning back. We run, lungs aching, overstretched, feet slipping on sodden leaves, our stumbling steps narrowly missing the overhanging trees.

"Faster!" I shout. The wind whistles and stirs the branches close behind us, but we can't outrun the rain and it hammers on our backs, hard and accusing.

You catch me up, your hair matted to red, clammy skin. You bend over, hands on knees, straining for air. When you look up you refuse to meet my eye.

Our feet pound down the hill, too fast to control our headlong descent until the slope eases and soaks up our staggering footsteps. The rain has cleared the village streets and all the doors are tightly closed. I find the house I'm looking for and bang my fist against the door, pressing one cold finger hard on the bell. I feel the swelling tide of panic, the tears threatening. I swallow hard and bang on the door again. Be in. Please be in. You're standing behind me, my little brother. I need to be stronger than this.

The door finally opens. He says nothing, merely stands aside to let us in. You go through to the kitchen where warmth and tea awaits. I turn to him. "He's up on the hillside, near the miner's hut. He's tied to a tree."

He asks no questions but pulls on his coat. He doesn't ask me to come with him. I start to think maybe this wasn't such a bad plan after all.

You sit huddled, knees up under our chin, as I ruffle the water from your hair with a towel. I want to tell you that you were brave, so much braver than me. But my throat is empty.

I close my eyes and try and imagine what is happening in the woods. The men of the village will find him with blood still dripping from his skull, his trousers loose. They will untie him, kick him, take him away. Maybe worse. I don't know. I don't even know what I want them to do. Just make him stop. Those men must know what he does to us boys, the secrets he has forced on their sons.

I can carry the guilt, the pain, balled up inside me. But his eyes turn towards my brother, my only flesh and blood. I know I need a plan. "Bring him up to the woods," I say to my brother. "Tempt him to his hunting ground. Don't worry, don't panic, I'll be waiting."

Now I see him coming, with his greedy eyes and hungry fingers. But I'm coming too, with wood crashing down on his combed black hair, cracking the grin off his face.

My hands shake, straining, pull the rope tighter.

"We need to hurry," I say, and we start to run.

A HALLOWEEN TALE

By Margaret Carruthers

The four boys stand at the broken gate, staring down the path at the tumbledown cottage with the paint flaking on the front door.

"My parents told me not to go down there," Russell says reluctantly, digging his toe into the crumbling mortar of the garden wall. "They say she's a witch, you know? She eats little boys alive. She got that Jason Stepney…"

"She did *not* get Jason Stepney," Tom insists. "His dad went to prison and his mum moved to Canada with him. Or the other way round." It had been two years ago, a lifetime at the age of nine. "I think she's a lonely old lady."

"I heard she has a snake," Dan supplies, his eyes wide.

"So what?" Tom asks. "My brother's got a snake."

"Your brother's got a corn snake, that's nothing." Jonathan's uncle works at the zoo, which makes him, naturally, an expert on all things that crawl and scuttle and slither. "I heard she's got a black mamba in there…"

"She so does not!" Tom punches Jonathan on the arm, hard enough to make him wince, and follows it up with two for flinching. "I reckon she's someone's grandma. I reckon she'll have tonnes of sweets."

Tonnes of sweets is a promising prospect. They have been trick or treating since seven. Now it's after nine, full dark, and their bags are bulging.

"Well, do we go in or not?" Tom asks the others. He's not chicken, even if they are.

"We've got plenty of sweets." Russell delves into his own pillowcase and pulls out a Twix, pushing his Hulk mask to the top of his head so he can eat it.

"You can never have too many sweets," Tom replies. There's no argument about that.

Bending, Tom plucks four blades of grass that are growing through the cracks in the pavement outside the gate. "We'll draw straws," he says, holding his hand out with the grass sticking out of his fist. "Everyone choose a blade of grass."

One at a time, his friends choose their blades, leaving one for Tom. His fist is closed tight around the thin green strand.

"Who has the shortest piece?" he says.

Russell unfurls his hand first. The other is still clenched around his Twix, and it's beginning to melt.

Jonathan and Dan open their hands at the same time, on a count of three, with Tom an instant behind. Tom has the shortest blade of grass. "Ok, I'll go," he says as he turns and opens the gate. "I'm not scared of some stupid old witch, even if she does have a snake. And I get all the sweets, right?"

Russell mumbles a chocolaty protest. Jonathan is silent, but Dan reaches out to give him a friendly punch on the arm.

Tom doesn't flinch. He stares down the dark path, then looks back at his friends, who grin at him. Jonathan sticks his tongue out, black-stained with liquorice. *Right*, Tom thinks, *I'll show them. I'm not afraid of the old biddy.*

Putting his left foot on the cracked, overgrown path, he walks up to the dirty green door and lifts the knocker, shaped like a lion's head. He lets go of the knocker and the noise vibrates through the house. He steps back, half-expecting to see clouds of bats fly out of the eaves, like in Batman, but all that happens is a few more flakes of paint detach from the eaves of the house and drift around his feet.

Feet shuffle down the corridor and stop at the door. It creaks open a few inches, and a wizened face peeps out, above a rattling chain. "What do you want?" the old lady asks, her voice as sharp as sherbet.

I won't run. She doesn't frighten me. She's just an old woman, a lonely old woman with no friends. Tom looks back, hoping his friends are impressed with his bravery, but behind him the gate is lost in darkness.

He finds his voice. "It's Halloween. Me and my friends are doing trick or treat, you know?" He indicates his Buzz Lightyear costume. So lame. He wanted to be Iron Man, but Dan had already bagsied Iron Man.

"I don't know what you mean by trick or treat. Where are your friends? Scared to come up the path, frightened I'll eat them, are they? I know what everyone says about me. Calling me a witch, telling their children I'll eat them, or worse. I don't eat children. I have children of my own, although they never visit."

She huffs. Her breath smells of the stuff his mum puts in the wardrobes to get rid of moths. "Got better things to do than visit their old mum. I get lonely though. Why don't you and your friends come in? If you're not frightened, that is!" She smiles unexpectedly, and it's as if her whole face has become illuminated now the scowl has gone. She looks more like a grandma now, and less like a mad old bag as she pushes the door to and releases the chain, opening it wider so he can see her properly in the dusty light from the hallway.

She's short for a grown-up, no taller than Tom, and she's wearing a shapeless dress and a battered shawl that could be any colour under the dirt. The smell of moth-stuff is stronger now; it seems to rise from her in clouds as she moves.

"I have lemonade and cake inside," she says. "Both homemade. I've never heard of trick or treating so you can tell me what I've been missing out on. I can find some coins for you all, if that counts, some farthings."

Tom wants to tell her they don't have farthings any more, but her eyes are so bright, so eager for company, that he thinks it will probably upset her. He offers her a smile.

"Yes, coins count. I'd love to come in. I'll ask my friends if they want to come too." He returns to the gate. He can see the path now, the moon must have come out, but when he looks up he can't see it.

"You were a long time standing by the door," Russell says, the instant Tom lays his hands on the wooden gate. "Who were you taking to?"

"The old woman who lives there. Didn't you see her?"

"No," Dan says. "We didn't even see the door open."

"We couldn't hardly see you," Jonathan adds." Let's get out of here. It's creepy."

"She's got lemonade, and cake…" Suddenly Tom wants his friends to visit the old lady, wants it so hard it burns in his gut. "Come on, she's really lonely. You *have* to come!"

Russell shakes his head. "You shouldn't take sweets and cake from strangers," he says.

"What have we been doing all night?" Tom rattles his bag of sweets, and a few Starburst escape and roll in the gutter.

"I don't know, Tom," Dan says, wide-eyed. "I think we should go home. We've got enough…"

"Well if you're too chicken to go in, you can just stay here. I'm not scared." Tom turns his back on his friends, deafens his ears to their pleas, and heads back up the path. The door stands open, and the old lady is waiting to invite him in. He casts one glance back over his shoulder, but the path is in darkness, and his friends have fled.

#

On every Halloween night now, Tom's parents put a wreath of red roses at the gate of the old cottage. The children of the village stay away. They say the witch got Tom Langford, or maybe he moved to a different school, or to Canada...

#

In the cottage, Tom and the old lady sit drinking homemade lemonade and eating cake by candlelight. She tells him about her children and shows him some farthings, and he drops jam down the front of his Buzz Lightyear costume. They chat for hours as, outside, the years pass.

HOUSE BLOOD

By Ian Millsted

I am house blood. The field blood call me soft, or lucky. They call me other things too. I was one of them once but that was before I was old enough to work the fields, before my lady chose me.

We are fewer, we house blood, than those of the field. We eat the food they grow and drink the ales they brew. They say all we do is serve the Lord and Lady. The Lord and Lady do not eat the food or drink the ale, for they have their own sustenance, but they require our assistance in all manner of things. We ready their clothes when they dress in the evening. We light the candles and lamps as is the fashion although, in truth, they don't need them. We saddle the horses or prepare the carriages for when they ride out to see other lords and ladies or to survey their property; both fields and field blood alike. We scrub the floors where the stains would run dark were they left. We clean and polish the golden cups.

The butler, senior of all the house blood, calls me manservant. My lady calls me boy. I believe I have lived through fifteen winters. I know for certain I have counted eight winters in the house since I was plucked from the field as I was about to start gathering in the harvest; a task field blood are usually first set to when they have passed seven or eight winters. My mother is no longer among the field blood. My father might be but I don't know who he is, or was. My lord would know, for he takes a great interest in the breeding of blood, but no servant ever asks such a question of their lord or lady.

When I was first taken into the house my duties were to do what tasks any of the other house blood required of me. I peeled and chopped vegetables in the kitchen for the cook. I helped polish the table and other furniture until it met the butler's approval. Most of my time was spent scrubbing floors and helping the maid feed the laundry through the mangle. There was always so much laundry.

I had been kept busy in all these tasks from harvest time through to the following summer when the butler informed me that I was to wait at table the next evening. He showed me how to wear the clothes of a manservant and said that I would get used to the tightness of the buttons done up to the top of my throat. He also told me what I could expect to see but I already knew. We all knew.

The lord and lady were expecting guests; of their own kind of course. I joined another manservant, some winters my senior, and we waited by the door to accept the cloaks of the visitors on their arrival. After we completed that first task the butler showed them into the Green Room where they were greeted by our own lord and lady. There were five in the visiting party: the lord and lady brought their daughter and there were two blood as well, two girls about the same age as my fellow manservant. They looked more like house blood than field blood to my eyes, although their skin appeared too soft to have served much in either capacity. Their lord bid them remove their cloaks, beneath which they wore simple white shift dresses. Although they did as they were asked their eyes barely registered any response.

"A gift for you, Lady Blaise," the visiting lord said as greetings were exchanged.

"Twins?" my lord asked. His guest nodded in confirmation.

"And red haired," said my lady. "You do us high honour."

"I've been keeping them back for the right time," said the guest. "They should be sweet indeed."

The two girls in white were directed to stand either side of the fireplace. Our lord and lady and their guests sat and talked of mutual friends and of the wider world I had never seen. They spoke of things they remembered, and seemed to miss, from when they were younger. The visitors' daughter joined in with all this even though she looked no more than five or six winters old. Her voice was childlike but her words were those of a much older person.

The three of us, the butler, the other manservant and I, stood still in the corners of the room all evening. My lord did not call for drink to be served as I had been told he probably would not. It was my lady who eventually called attention once more to the twin girls.

"Now, I think we must share this gift you brought us, before you depart."

The visiting lord called the two girls to step forward into the middle of the room. He offered his hand to help my lady out of her chair and guided her to one of the twins.

"Our hostess first, I think," he said.

My lady wore one of her finest gowns; crimson velvet and full to the floor. She walked once around the girl who was standing stock still save for her barely perceptible breathing. She gently touched a spot on the girl's neck and then, slowly and carefully, she put her lips to the place she had chosen. She spread them wider, before biting into the girl's skin. Two trickles of blood ran down the girl's neck and shoulder, chasing each other like raindrops on a window. They ran inside her shift and I watched, doing nothing, as eventually I saw the blood drip to the floor.

My lord had, by now, joined my lady to feast, although choosing to do so at the veins on the opposite side of the girl's neck. Our guests commanded the other girl to kneel so that their daughter could reach to bite her neck. Her parents knelt to join her in feeding.

There was no conversation while our masters drank. They made no loud noises as a field blood might when sucking a pear or apple. The room was hideously serene.

The young daughter had her fill first and sat back; a delighted, blood-stained smile on her face. The four adults kept feeding until their victims collapsed to the floor, whereupon the masters returned to their chairs and continued their banal conversations. When the guests got up to leave they stepped over the bodies as if they were not there. Our own lord and lady retired to their room upstairs, something they did not often do, and the butler instructed myself and the other manservant to remove the bodies. I lifted the first body by the legs as my fellow servant lifted her shoulders and we carried her to one of the outbuildings where a large, rough box was waiting ready. As we walked back to get the other one, he nodded up at the light shining from a first floor window.

"We'll not need to worry about any more orders for a couple of hours," he said.

I must have looked puzzled. He laughed, I think at me.

"It's the only time he can get hard, is when he's freshly drunk blood."

Though young, I knew enough of animal mating to understand what he meant. I knew also that the field blood coupled for pleasure as well as to mate, but this new knowledge about my lord showed me for the first time that there was a weakness in our masters.

\#

I remained the youngest of the house blood for five more winters. As I became proficient at all my duties more tasks were assigned to me. All sorts of practical knowledge was passed down from senior servant to junior while the master occasionally offered advice but never lowered himself to tackle any tasks. I learned how to harness and lead the horses for the carriage when the lord or lady wanted to visit neighbours, although the older manservant did this task most often. I cleaned glasses until they were pristine and I did the same for the ornate glass decorations that hung from the centre of each ceiling. I learned how to maintain and repair the mechanisms of house. When still young and new, I asked the butler about the tubes of soft, white matter that ran along some corners and down several walls. He said those were from the days when rooms were lit by something called electricity rather than candles. I started to see a different house all around me.

The lord and lady, and the frequent guests they had, conducted themselves for the most part as if we house blood were not there. While the butler was ever vigilant to keep male and female servants away from each others sleeping rooms – "We'll have none of you behaving like rutting field blood in this house" – the lord and lady thought nothing of summoning any servant to their chambers. When the lady wanted to bathe, then the two maids, as well as the older manservant and myself, had to carry a succession of hot kettles full of water upstairs until she was satisfied with the temperature. At that point one of the maids would help her undress and step into the bath while the rest of us waited in case she wanted fresh hot water brought. I had seen nothing abnormal in this when I first worked at the house but as I grew and my body changed I found it increasingly difficult yet fascinating. If my mistress noticed my unease she showed no indication. They enjoyed flaunting their power over us.

While life in the house was largely routine and laborious there were occasional incidents that were clearly unexpected, even to those servants who had been there for many years. I was lighting a fire in the library where the lord was studying old maps when our lady stormed in and the two of them, quite oblivious to my presence, shouted at each other in a way I had never previously heard.

"Is it true?"

"Is what true?"

"You've made another."

"Who told you that?"

"So, it is true?"

"What of it?"

"What were you thinking?"

"Perhaps that a lord should be able to do what he wants."

"And if we all did that, what would happen then? You know the land, the population of blood, won't sustain it. How could you be so selfish?"

"It's nothing. Nobody need know."

"I know! And if I found out then others will. Who was it this time? Another of the field blood catch your eye?"

"She's no one. I'll sort it out."

"Better tell the boy here to sharpen your sword. Wouldn't want to make a mess of the decapitation, would we?"

Lord Blaise noticed me. "I'll get my sword, he can saddle my horse." This was said with some distain, but he continued. "In fact he can get the carriage ready. You'll come with me, boy."

The lord drove the carriage but insisted I go with him, sitting alongside him instead of standing on the backboard as would have been usual. He remained silent for most of the journey until we reached the top of a cliff below which I could see a narrow, muddy river. I had not travelled this far from the house before. There were a few buildings but most looked empty or had vegetation growing into or through them.

"Are you feeling brave, boy?"

I said nothing, assuming my assent was not really being sought or, indeed, that it would make any difference if I said no. We were approaching a thin strip of track that reached across the emptiness to more land on the far side of the valley. It became obvious we were going to go across. I could see the track was held up somehow by chains or cables but I felt my fear rising all the same. The lord slowed the pace slightly but guided the horses onto the track. I heard something creak but I fixed my eyes straight ahead, willing us to be back on solid ground. The whole thing must have taken moments but time seemed to slow. Once we got to the far side, I realised I had been holding my breath. I let it go. My lord looked across at me and smiled, but to himself, not me.

Not long after, we arrived at a small building shrouded by trees. My lord pulled the horses to a halt and jumped down, ordering me to follow. He opened the door, clearly expecting it to be unlocked, and walked straight in. The inside was too dark for me to see but my master, for whom the dark was no barrier, seemed to walk in a straight line and I followed as best as my hearing would allow. When he opened another door a little light shone into what I now saw was a central corridor. Inside the lit room were three large armchairs and a sofa. Upon the sofa, half sitting and half prone, was a pallid woman wearing the dress of a lady. The dress did not fit and as she moved to acknowledge my lord the material fell off one shoulder to reveal most of one breast. She had none of the undergarments I had seen on my lady.

"Blaise," she whispered. Her smile, as she recognised my lord, was open enough for me to see that she was not blood.

"I am still weak, Blaise."

"It will pass." My lord offered her his hand, which she took and used to bring herself, slowly, to her feet. "You must feed in order to gain your true strength."

On hearing this, the woman looked at me, her eyes widening. I looked across to my lord who fixed his eyes directly on mine. I tried, vainly, to look away.

"Take off your jacket, boy."

I was compelled, not just in the way of a dutiful servant, but physically. I removed my jacket and dropped it onto one of the chairs. My lord then commanded me to unbutton my collar and top button of my shirt. Again, I did so. The woman stepped closer to me and stared at my neck. She was reaching out to touch my throat when my lord broke off eye contact with me. Before I could move, a sword flashed through the air and cleaved straight through the neck of the woman before me. She toppled over but her head, detached and with eyes still open, hit the floor first. I was surprised at how little blood flowed. My lord picked up the head, by the hair, and threw it onto the fire.

"You will speak of this to no one," he said as we drove back to the house. After some minutes he added, "There are masters and there are blood. There are no true bridges from one to the other".

That night, in bed, I thought about my mother.

#

The arrival of a new kitchen maid displaced my position as the youngest servant. The girl was not, as was usually the case, a young field blood who caught the attention of the lord and lady, but a gift from another house. Her main tasks were to run the errands the cook avoided; bringing in eggs and milk and taking out scraps and waste. She was alert and learned her duties quickly. When she had been in the house one season I walked into the library, to empty the ashes from the fireplace, to find her looking at one of the books from the master's shelf.

"Put it back," I said, more in fear for myself if the master found me in there with the books disturbed, than out of concern for the newcomer. "Servants are forbidden to touch the books."

She put the book back on the shelf. "Do you know what's in them?" she asked.

"Words," I shrugged.

"Knowledge," she said. "Can you read?"

I told her that, of course, I could not.

"I can teach you."

She walked from the room and I checked to see that there was no sign of the books having been disturbed. The master rarely looked at them but he was protective all the same.

I was chopping firewood behind one of the outhouses when the girl next tried asking me questions.

"What is your name?"

"I was called Ben when I was a field blood, but the lord and lady don't like us using names."

"I'm Mary," she said. She picked up a stick and scratched some lines in the mud. "That's a letter. A bee, sounds like ber, like in your name, Ben. I can teach you. I think you'll learn quickly. I've watched you. You see more than most of the blood here."

"The masters won't like it."

She rubbed out the marks in the ground and smiled at me. "They won't know."

Finding the opportunity to learn my letters proved easier than I thought. I was trusted, by now, and we were both of us too unimportant for anyone to be bothered about. We completed our duties quicker than the others and stole what time we could. Mary found some old, tattered books in one of the outbuildings and showed me how the letters went together to make sounds and how the sounds formed into words. When we were both another winter older I was able to read many of the books.

When the lord and lady went to visit others of their kind, Mary and I dared more. On one occasion we crept into the library and found books which showed the world before the masters. I think Mary knew some of this already but to read of schools and hospitals, cars and trains opened my mind. The masters had not always ruled and perhaps they would not always do so. My lord and lady did not age, but I had seen how one made could be killed.

We also walked further away from the house. The other house blood must have known we were away but probably assumed we were seeking privacy to satisfy our lusts. Only the butler would have been bothered and he was not as alert as he had been. The rest would expect us to get caught and punished accordingly.

We tried to find the remains of some of the things we had seen or read about in the books. I told Mary of the bridge but it was too far away. We found an empty building that still had a roof and we moved some of the books there to protect them. The building itself already held many books, although most of them seemed to be the same. Mary said she had been shown this book by the woman who had taught her to read. She read some of it to me; an odd story about a man who offered his own blood to friends and lived after death but in a way unlike the masters.

Where I had once disliked going on errands among the field blood, I now anticipated each opportunity to see the world beyond the house and compare it to the images in the books. More and more I could see the evidence for a previous world. There was an old tower still standing, overlooking the field where most of the Blaise field blood laboured. The door was old and gave way when I pushed it. From the top of the tower I could see a wide track and in the distance another bridge – I knew what they were now – spanning what must have been an even greater break in the land. I wondered what lay on the other side. Was there somewhere that the masters did not rule or control?

I arrived back from my errands one day to be called into the drawing room. My lord and lady were sat in two separate chairs with Mary standing facing them, reading from a book. She shot me a quick warning glance but in doing so gave us away, for my lady spotted her.

"Ah, boy," said my lord. "Fetch a glass of water for the girl. We wouldn't want her mouth to get too dry while she amuses us with her reading."

I brought the water and set it on a table near Mary. My lord gestured for me to remain so I went to stand in the corner. I listened as Mary continued reading what seemed to be a nonsensical book about talking rabbits trying to escape a farmer. The book was not large and Mary soon finished.

My lady commanded me to step forward. I watched as she took a pen and wrote some words on a sheet of paper. Even knowing that she was trying to get me to reveal my new education I couldn't stop my face reacting as I read the words "I know what happened to your mother" on the paper she held in front of my eyes.

My lord rose from his chair and stood in front of Mary. She tried to look away but he grabbed her by the chin and held her, forcibly, where he could meet her eyes. Mary's eyes remained open but she was no longer looking at anything in the room. My lord walked around her, taking his time to pick the spot where he would bite. I moved toward them but my lady rose and held me in place. "Be still," she whispered as she looked at me.

Unable to move, I watched as Mary, the girl who gave me knowledge, was robbed of her life's blood. In my mind I stepped forward to save Mary but my body was powerless. When they were done my lord turned to me and said "There are masters and there are blood. There is nothing else."

I am house blood. I scrub the floors. I clean the carriage. I polish the goblets. And I take particular pride in keeping a keen edge on my master's sword.

LATITUDE

By Pete Sutton

I'm packing for my journey. It's across Britain between the northern latitudes of 51 and 52 degrees, give or take. From the west coast, because I live in Bristol and can get dropped off there, to the east coast. This will take me through the Prime Meridian. Two mates are coming with me, and I've got three weeks off work to do this. I considered doing it for charity, but the pressure! So instead it's just to prove I can do it.

Tommy is driving us to Portishead, our start position zero, and then we're going to walk to Dover, because that's on the coast and has good travel links. Obviously. Andy and Rob are coming with me. Andy is a solid bloke, Rob I'm not so sure about. I've spent a small fortune on all the proper gear. This is to be my first solo adventure, well, it's with the lads but I mean it's my first holiday without the family since forever. This is a test. Can I do it? It'll be nice to get away from it all.

I've been using Google a lot to get this right, maps, Earth, Wikipedia and all sort of interesting sites. Spent more time on this than on the day job, if I'm honest. Although that's not such a bad thing, is it? Work to live and all that. Everything is in place. I have planned the trip to the nth degree. Well to the 51st degree, really.

#

It's an 8am start and I'm up at seven, eager, excited, nervous. The doorbell goes at seven thirty. It's Andy.

"Alright mate, ready for the off?"

"Yep, fancy a cuppa?"

We head into the kitchen, and Andy screws his nose up.

"What's with all these flies?"

"It was so hot last night I left the window open. Came down this morning to find 'em all over the house."

"No fly spray?"

"Nope. And no time to buy any. I guess they'll die off when they run out of food. Things usually do."

Andy blows a fly from the rim of his mug and takes a sip. "Seen Rob?" he asks.

"Not yet. Bit early for him, isn't it?"

"Tommy will get here next, I bet."

It's a bet I don't take, because it's a sure thing. Andy has also spent a ton on the kit. His bright red rucksack sits next to mine in the hall. We are camping, we've both invested in the cheapest, lightest tent we can and a mat to make the ground softer. I've also splashed out on a silky sleeping bag. We're going to have to forage at shops though, we're not outdoorsy types. I'm in my mid-forties and I'm not looking forward to sleeping on the ground. We might break it up with B&B's. Actually, we're likely to break it up with B&B's. This is all practice for future travels. A proof of concept, as they say in work. There's a knock on the door.

"Alright, Tommy? Come in, the kettle's on."

"Ready for the off?" Tommy snatches at a stray fly.

"Yarp," I say.

"Rob not here?"

"Not yet. He'll miss his cup of tea if he's much later."

"Well, I'll skip the sugar, if you don't mind," he says, looking at the sugar bowl which has turned into an all you can eat buffet for the flies.

"Yeah, sorry about that." I shrug.

"Have you phoned Chloe yet?"

Chloe is my wife, sorry, ex-wife, mother of my children – Olivia, twelve and Mace, ten. Yes, I lost the battle over naming them.

"Not yet mate, she'll be getting the kids to school. I'll give her a call later, when we're on the road."

"She at her mother's still? I've not seen her since she moved out," says Tommy. He always had a bit of a thing about Chloe, though if I asked him he'd deny it.

I nod.

"You have told her you're doing this, haven't you?"

"Not as such. I did say I'd be away for a while so I won't be able to take the kids at the weekend."

"Jesus man, this is why your marriage imploded!" Andy chimes in. It's not news, not to me.

"I know, I know, but you know, she's just..." I flail around for the words. They both look sympathetic.

At seven fifty the doorbell rings.

"Alright Rob, we're just packing the car." I hustle the other two out and pile the rucksacks into the boot of Tommy's car. Rob looks sheepish, and I notice for the first time that he doesn't have a rucksack. "Yours still in your car?"

"Look mate, I, er, well that is..." He takes a deep breath. "I'm not coming."

"What? Everything's set, we're just about to head off!"

"For fuck's sake, Rob." Andy fiddles angrily with his rucksack.

I sigh, trying to conceal the fact that I'm just as annoyed. Trust Rob to mess things up at the last minute. "What's the story, Rob?"

"Well I don't think I can afford it, and three weeks is a long time to be away from the missus, and I haven't got the right kit and ..."

"Right, fine," I interrupt, taking a deep breath. Andy is still intent on the fastening of his rucksack, Tommy is staring into his tea, refusing to meet Rob's eye. The flies buzz lazily in the background. I kick my own bag, then lump it up onto my back. Rob's a jerk, but he's not worth spoiling the adventure for. "You can come pick us up in Dover, then. Save us spending a fortune on the train. It's only fair."

Rob nods, a bit reluctantly. "OK, it's the least I can do."

I come to a fast decision. "Look, come round tonight anyway, in fact, take my spare key and you can get rid of the flies, get us some tinnies and get dinner on. I'll text you our progress."

As we drive off he stands looking after us, digging the toe of his trainer into the gravel on the path. Tommy speeds off, no lingering goodbyes are necessary. I wonder if I've done the right thing, giving him access to the house. I try and concentrate on the trip and not worry about things at home. At least, not until later.

"Fuck him." Andy gives his judgement in a low tone. I sigh.

"Why d'you invite him around tonight?"

"Not sure, just felt right."

"Jesus Mal, you always make allowances for him."

I can only agree, and Andy snorts in derision before moving on to discussing the first day's walk. We're actually sleeping at mine tonight, it's about twelve miles from Portishead to my house. It's important we go coast to coast though. And take the rucksacks to see if we can walk the distance whilst carrying them. This entire trip is to see if I can do it.

I'm planning on leaving it all behind, you see.

The trip has started with a bit of a downer but we're planning to set a pace of twelve miles per day, so it will take us sixteen days to reach Dover. With four days contingency, that's all the holiday I can take from work. My out of office reads – 'I'm so far away from my desk and phone you'll never be able to contact me. I'll be living it slow walking from coast to coast.' Plus all the usual – 'in case of emergency call blah blah blah.' But there are never any emergencies in work. They probably won't even notice I'm not there.

Tommy drops us off, shakes our hands as though we were really off on an adventure and drives off without looking back. It's just us and the open road now. Although we do go and dip our toes in the sea first. Well you have to, don't you, on coast to coast walks? Picking up my pack for the first time, I realise it's going to feel heavier and heavier as we go along but right now it feels good on my back. From the Battery Point Light we wave goodbye to the Severn Estuary and head back towards my house.

We shoot the shit as we walk along.

"So what was the real reason the wife took the kids and left?" Andy asks me after an hour or so of conversation. I can tell he's been dying to ask me.

"Fuck mate, what's the real reason behind anything?"

"Were you sleeping around? Drinking too much? Gambling?"

"Nothing like that. I'm not an alcoholic or anything, although I think we'll be sinking a few pints on this trip, yeah? None of the other crap either. Although you know money's been tight?"

"How come? You earn a good crust, so does she. Doesn't she?"

"Yeah, but it was always, the kids need this, the house needs that, we need to go on holiday."

We are crossing the M4 at the Easton-In-Gordano roundabout and the noise of the traffic and the need to concentrate on crossing roads forces us into silence for a bit. My phone buzzes as we cross. Andy's obviously does too, as we both pull them out on the other side.

What's with all the flies?

I text Rob back.

"Dunno. Can you get rid for us pleez?"

Andy types something longer. "Ready?" I ask. He grunts in reply and we start off again as he puts his phone away.

"You going to give her a call?" he eventually asks me. I take my phone out and look at it.

"Not just yet," I say.

We carry on walking down the A369 towards the Clifton suspension bridge. It's pretty much all countryside for a while. Cars zip past, doing our full days walk in thirty minutes. But the people inside will be impoverished, they don't get the smells, they can't linger over the sights, they don't get the tactile feel of the road eaten up step by step. I envy them a tiny bit at the moment. Sometimes when I set out on a holiday I want to skip to the end. At least, I always used to. This though, this is what I've been planning for ages, been looking forward to. Freedom from the office, the family, responsibilities. I remind myself to cheer the fuck up. Andy is texting again.

"You remember the holidays you took as a kid?" I ask him.

"Sure. Godawful things. Always in Britain. Spending hours driving to some arse end of nowhere, getting lost, parents arguing, weather crap."

"Idyllic childhood memories."

We laugh.

"I ever tell you about almost dying on holiday?" I ask.

"No?" Andy looks up from his phone, suddenly more interested.

"I was in Cornwall, at the seaside. Insipid English sunshine, but we didn't know any better. My parents bought me a dinghy, blew it up on the beach, launched it out into the waves. Spent ages paddling about."

"What happened? Get caught in a riptide?"

"Nah, that would have been more exciting. The bloody thing

burst. Had to swim miles back to shore, and I'm not a great swimmer. Parents didn't even notice until I flopped down next to them. Knackered me out. For some reason I'd swum back with the paddle but let the dinghy sink. Bastard shop owner didn't even give them a refund."

"So by almost die, what you actually mean is 'had to swim for a bit.'" Andy grinned.

"I could have drowned! What if I couldn't swim? This last year my life has felt a bit like that moment, you know. Scudding over the waves, sun shining, having fun… Then a bang and I'm flailing and trying not to drown."

Andy just shakes his head and pulls out his phone, yet again.

"Someone hassling you?" I ask.

"Nah."

"OK. Let's stop for a pint at The George?"

He nods, still fiddling with his phone, I'm starting to get irritated. I plan on taking it off him at the pub and changing the language to Chinese or something.

"You ever wonder about the whole north-south thing?" I ask.

"Eh?"

"Well, if you go far enough north all directions become south." I try to explain.

"Wow that's some profound shit, or shit profundity. I can't tell which." He looks at me, his eyebrows raised. I'm not sure he gets it.

"It's just this whole trip. It's arbitrary really. Following imaginary lines. We may as well have circumnavigated Bristol or climbed a mountain."

"What are you trying to say?"

Unable to tell if he's being deliberately dense, I decide to drop it. "Dunno really. Let's go get that pint."

"If you circumnavigated Bristol, would you do the unitary authority or the actual city?" Andy asks. "What counts as Bristol and not Bristol? You know, with South Glos starting a couple of streets away from you."

"Not sure. I'd have to plan it. Perhaps we should do that next year?"

He gives me a strange look. "Sure," he says eventually. "Next year…"

His phone buzzes. I'm tempted to snatch it out of his hands and throw it into the traffic. Instead I glance over his shoulder. It's a text from Rob. There's a picture, but it's dark and fuzzy.

"What's that?" I say.

"Rob taking pictures of the inside of his pocket? He's a spanner."

I give him a ring. He doesn't answer. I ring the home phone, and it goes through to that annoying woman's voice. I've been meaning to change that. Would Rob listen to the answerphone if I left a message? I hang up and send him another text instead. I take a picture of the road going down to the George. I know it's coming up on the right, but I can't see its cream walls yet. *"first stop"* I text.

"Right, let's hope it's opening time," I say. Andy just grins in reply. At the pub I wait for Andy to go to the toilet, knowing he'll leave his phone on the table. He always does. I snatch it up and try to guess the code. Birthday? Well that was easy. I read the texts. It's a whole conversation with Rob.

"What's with all the flies?"

"I know, that's weird right? Like smthing has died somewhere? Did you notice the smell too?"

"There's a lot of air fresheners?"

"Have a look about whilst you're there."

"There's an odd smell upstairs, think it's coming from the attic, you

know where he keeps his ladder?"

"No idea, in that disaster he calls a shed?"

"What are you doing?" Andy has come back quicker than I expected, his face drawn into a frown.

"I was going to change the language on your phone, as a joke." I hold my hands up, all innocence. "You caught me, I guess that means it's my round." I click off the message app and onto the settings and hand it back to him.

Andy picks up his phone and spends some time staring at it and prodding it while I'm at the bar. We sink the next pint in embarrassed silence. I'm a bit worried about Rob. Perhaps I shouldn't have given him a key. That's the problem with snap decisions – they come back to bite you on the arse later.

"Right this walk isn't going to finish itself," I say, downing the dregs of my pint and getting to my feet. "Let's go."

"I think whoever designed my shoes hates feet," Andy complains, pocketing his ever-present phone.

"Blister?"

"Think so. Afraid to look, will have to limp on."

"Told you to break those boots in." I try not to sound smug and fail dismally.

"I did!" he protests. "I wore them round the house and to work."

"Maybe you're wearing the wrong socks then?"

"Yeah, maybe. I have some blister plasters in the bag, maybe I should put them on now?"

He walks off to the toilet with his rucksack. This time he takes his phone with him. I spend the time reading Facebook and Twitter. When he comes back he doesn't seem to be limping. Although I don't remember seeing him limp at all.

"Ready?"

"Yarp."

I wave to the bar maid as we leave; she is reading a newspaper and barely acknowledges.

In a short while we are at the mid-way point, the Clifton suspension bridge. Half way over I stop and look down. Andy follows my gaze, down into the waters that churn at the bottom of the gorge.

"They say that if you jump you end up suffocating in the mud, you don't drown and unless you hit the rocks the fall probably won't kill you."

"Need to phone the Samaritans, mate?" He looks like he's only half joking.

"Nah. Come on, we'll be home in a couple of hours and we can have pies and ale."

He checks his phone as we walk off.

"Expecting a call?" I ask.

"Yeah, can't get in touch with Rob. I wanted him to get me some stuff from the chemist for when we get to yours, some antiseptic cream. Wouldn't want my blister to get infected."

It seems plausible. And yet...

We walk up the hill from the bridge, past the zoo and towards the downs and the top of Whiteladies Road. We are chuffing a bit by the time we get there.

"Another pint?" I ask. Andy nods enthusiastically.

"Port of Call," I say and we head down the hill to the pub, which is tucked away in a small alleyway off the main road. Andy gets them in.

"Want to tell me anything?" I ask, as he dumps the two pints on the tables.

"Like what?"

"Like what you and Rob are talking about. You discussing me?"

"A little bit." He stares into the depths of his pint. "Look, we're a bit worried about you, mate."

"Worried as in anxious about my problems? Or worried as in disturbed?"

"Er... The first one." He looks like he wants the table to open up and swallow him, pint, phone and all.

"Relax," I tell him. "I'm not about to do something stupid."

"Ok. Ok. But you know we're your friends and we're here for you, yeah?"

"Yeah."

There's an awkward silence. I decide to fill it.

"When we get to Dover let's just carry on, yeah? Let's walk around the globe at the 51st parallel. It goes through a bunch of countries I've always wanted to visit. It'll be ... what?"

"What what?"

"Why're you looking at me that way?" I demand.

"What way?"

"Like I've sprouted an extra head."

"Didn't realise I was. Sorry." He doesn't look sorry. "Look, I've only got the three weeks off by agreeing to work Christmas. I can't go gallivanting off round the world. And neither can you. Although they don't live with you any more, you've still got a family relying on you."

I sigh. "Yeah, you're right. Another pint?"

Waiting at the bar, I can see Andy out of the corner of my eye. He's on the phone again, paying no attention to me. As I open my wallet to pay I glance at the ferry ticket inside. He's right, I still have responsibilities.

While we drink the next pint I make sure we talk about proper

English subjects, cricket, weather, the goddamn coalition, beer and other such profundities. From Whiteladies we skirt Cotham and the Montpelier/St Paul's border, cross the M32 at J3 and join Stapleton Road, once the most dangerous road in Bristol, and possibly the country. Today it's buzzing with BBQs and folk having a good time. When we get to the railway bridge we stop to get ice creams at the corner shop. Only a few miles left to go, and we need a bit of a lift, and a cool down. At Eastville Park Andy gives up trying to be surreptitious and phones Rob.

"Oy! Answer your phone," he says eventually. I'm guessing to the voicemail. He tries again, my house number probably. Still no reply, I guess, apart from the woman on my answerphone.

"We're almost there anyway." I say. "It's the end of stage one and the beginning of the rest of the journey."

He nods, indicating we should move on.

"I've been thinking about my next trip." I say. "There's about forty places called Bristol, most of them are in the States. I'd like to visit them all. Get away from it all."

"Sounds interesting."

"Yeah, there's a couple in Canada too, I could do them on the same trip. I'd have to do the ones in Barbados, Costa Rica, Jamaica and Peru on a separate trip."

"Sounds like you've been planning to get away for a while?"

"Yeah ever since … well you know. With Chloe and the kids and all."

"You haven't phoned her yet."

I wonder why he's so keen I phone my ex-wife. "No, not yet. She'll be at work. I'll phone her later."

We hit Fishponds Road. The home stretch.

"You know, I hardly ever go to south Bristol." I say, to steer the conversation away from Chloe. "Why do you think that is?"

"Well it's obvious, innit?"

"Is it?"

"Yeah. You're a filthy northerner and the north calls you. It's in your blood, isn't it?"

"You may as well say that I was born in the west and therefore the west calls to me, but I live on the east side of the city."

"North is more of an identity thing though, isn't it?" he says.

I've never really thought of it that way before. We walk past all the familiar sights. I think it's time to move on, but I'm circling the centre of gravity which is the home I bought for the family. When we get there and I open the door there's no sign of Rob. There are, if anything, more flies. I deposit Andy in the kitchen and grab him a beer from the fridge before I head upstairs.

The ladder is directly below the attic. I climb it reluctantly, one step at a time. They are still where I left them. Still chained. Rob must have thought they were being held against their will or something. The sawdust and newspaper glistens red under the single bare bulb. I hoped Chloe would have kept them sated for longer. I wonder again what will happen next time they run out of food. I'm careful not to get too close. Rob's phone buzzes, and I snatch it up and switch it off. I listen for noises from downstairs, but it sounds like Andy is still in the kitchen. I hear the fridge door close, the buzzing of the flies…

Mace glares at me. I know I've done wrong but why does he hate me so? Olivia is more needy.

"You won't leave us, Daddy?" she asks, in a small voice. Her mouth is so red. I shake my head, but my hand touches the pocket with my wallet in, and the promise of escape.

UNCLE LUCAS

By Clare Dornan

I crept behind the men, who were laughing loudly like they always did. I heard Uncle Lucas telling his jokes and everyone howled and their shoulders shook, they were laughing so much. It was about a dog chasing a cat that got killed by a truck. I didn't get the joke.

I sneaked between the legs of the men until I could see Uncle Lucas sitting on the crates in the middle of the garage. Everyone froze when they saw me, except Uncle Lucas. He smiled and said, "Hey little man, you wanna join the party?"

I looked up to him and said, "Why is it so funny?"

No one said anything until Uncle Lucas called out, "Hey, Red, tell my nephew here, why it's so funny?" I turned round and saw Red turn red.

"It's the way you tell 'em, Lucas," he said, and everyone started laughing again.

Uncle Lucas ruffled my hair and winked at me. "You just think about it," he said, "and let me know when you've worked it out."

#

Mama always said that it was Uncle Lucas who looked out for us, took good care of us. Uncle Lucas is mama's little brother, and, man, he sure is little. He's even smaller than she is. He'd come round for dinner and we'd play-fight in the living room 'til mama finally got annoyed and told us to stop. But I knew she wasn't really angry because she let us do it every time.

Mama asked me to help Uncle Lucas deliver and pick up things he needed. So I'd do small jobs for him at the weekends and he'd often ruffle my hair and say, "do you know why it's funny yet?" and I'd say, "no, I'm still thinking."

It kind of became our thing.

#

One summer I started working for him, helping out in the office. I'd show people up to his room and he'd tell them I was his nephew and then they'd be really friendly. Sometimes they brought him things, cakes and presents, like it was his birthday, but it never was. Uncle Lucas would always start joking, and they'd start laughing but there was one guy sitting by the door who never joined in. And this guy was huge. I never heard him say anything and Uncle Lucas never told me who he was.

It wasn't long before I realised Uncle Lucas wasn't as nice to everyone else as he was to me. The door to his room was so thick I could never hear what was going on inside, but some of the people who came in the front went out another way. "He's like a pit bull on heat when he's angry," I heard someone say.

At the end of the day, Uncle Lucas would sometimes come into the office and he'd shout across to me.

"Hey kid, do you know why it's funny yet?"

And even though my head was swimming with questions I'd only ever say, "no, still thinking."

#

When summer finished and it was time for school, I knocked on his door and said my thank-yous as mama had taught me. Then I said I didn't think I could work for him again, which I knew would make mama mad.

He nodded slowly, and shrugged. "Did you ever work out why it's funny?" he asked.

I suddenly just had to tell him. I said, "It's not funny, Uncle

Lucas. None of your jokes are funny. Everyone just laughs because they're scared of you."

He stood up, all five foot four of him. He came eye to eye with me and said, "that's the joke, kid. That a short arse like me can make all those guys laugh just because I tell them to." Then he started laughing, his big, loud, belly laugh. But I didn't join in.

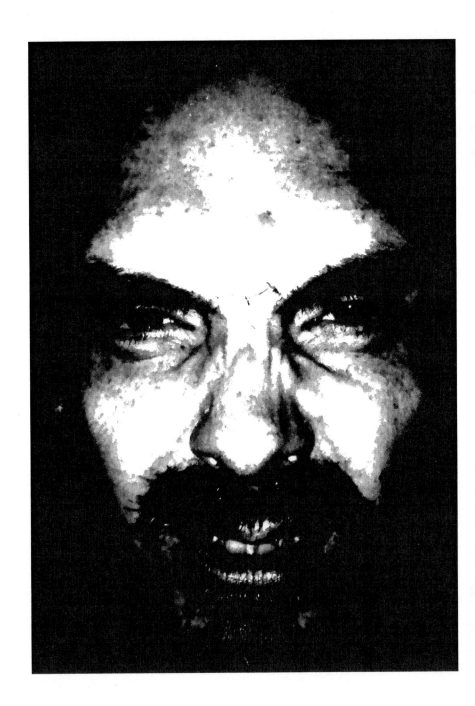

HATER

By Pete Sutton

T he buzzer under his finger vibrated slightly as the bell rang inside. It was one of those bells he could stand and press and keep pressing. He preferred them over the ones that just played a few notes, although both could cause irritation if used correctly. He was early; the Monday nighters, because they met at each other's houses, disliked people arriving early more than people arriving late. Susan opened the door. He had noted down in his writer's journal about Susan – 'Bored housewife type, sad erotic daydreams masquerading as fiction, best tactic either faint praise or over-enthusiasm using a possible paedophile-like persona.'

"Oh it's you … you're a little early … come in … do you want a drink?" Susan showed him to the dining room where the table was set up for the meeting, and bustled off to the kitchen. When she brought him his drink there was an awkward five minutes of conversation until she excused herself to check on the oven. The bell rang, a quick, polite buzz.

"Can you get that please?" Susan shouted from the back of the house.

Richard stood on the doorstep and Michael and Julie were walking up the road. He spotted them over Richard's shoulder, and they saw him, but Richard was oblivious. He let the newcomer in and closed the door, following him into the dining room. The bell went again.

"Your turn," he said to Richard, who had just sat down.

For Richard he had in his journal: 'Wannabe travel writer, had some success with short stories. Encourage him to send stories and manuscripts to publishers that demand a greater level of quality and talent. Each rejection will add another nail in the coffin of his ambition.'

Richard, Michael and Julie enthusiastically greeted each other at the door and Susan hurried back into the room with a plate full of cakes.

"Are any of those cakes vegan?" he asked, knowing they wouldn't be, that Susan would feel guilty for not providing something special for him.

"Ah no, I'm afraid not."

It was Julie's turn to do a reading and everyone else's to provide criticism. For Julie he had: 'Possibly a lesbian, bit manly, short stories and poetry, actually has a modicum of talent, use harsher criticism than necessary. Emotional instability?'

Julie read her latest story that she thought 'could do with tightening up a bit.' It was actually quite interesting, about a creepy nightmare in the style of M R James. Predictably Michael, who he suspected was trying to get into Julie's pants, loved it. For Michael he had 'Science Fiction wannabe novelist, too nerdy for this group and can therefore be isolated as an outsider, make sure to use lots of allusions to classical literature, as he has never read anything that doesn't have aliens or elves in it.'

It was his turn to provide criticism.

"Well, Julie, there's a thin line between homage and plagiarism and I think you may have strayed across it. Although M R James is popular, he's a bit passé. I notice you've written it in first person, do you think third person point of view would improve it? I also thought the prose was a little purple, but I'm not sure if that was because you were too slavish in your aping of James? The core idea is just about OK and there are some parts that lifted it above the mundane, so I'd recommend a full rewrite."

It was moments like this, watching Julie's face as she struggled to cope with her crushed expectations, that he lived for. The others tried to follow with praise, but against his attack they sounded like they were trying to be too nice.

The rest of the evening passed as expected. When the discussion came up about the idea of an anthology they planned to self-publish, he presented a number of reasons why this was a bad idea.

When it came to leaving he tried to be last, to overstay his welcome enough to be plausibly nice and friendly without being overly creepy. Susan made it clear that he had to leave as Richard had also stayed behind. Eventually he thought the atmosphere was such that he'd spoiled the evening enough and was in danger of over-egging it.

He smiled as he walked home, picturing Susan and Richard talking about him, and he was happy with the mental image. They were all too nice in the group. He knew they'd be too polite to ask him to leave unless his behaviour became much worse; he kept it just the right side of what they would deem unacceptable. Once he'd overheard Julie talking to Susan after he'd ripped a previous story of hers apart. Julie was upset and must have said something about how unfair he was. Susan defended him, it wasn't his fault he was a 'little abrasive' and that he was 'very supportive of Richard' and her own work. That tickled him, he knew that his tactics were sound. Julie's answer was less impressive; she claimed he was 'over forty and a talentless loser' that had never, and never would get, one of 'his crappy monotonous stories' published. It rankled because it was true. The best sort of critique. Remembering that wiped the smile off his face.

He took his mobile out and checked the calendar; his next writer's meeting was on Thursday with the library group. He really enjoyed the library group. It had an essence of Alcoholics Anonymous, sitting on uncomfortable chairs in a big circle and taking turns to say how much they hated each other's work. He liked the fact that there were a couple of other Haters there. It added spice. He warmed himself on the memory of Julie holding back her tears as he told her that her work had crossed the line into plagiarism. A job well done, he thought.

NORTH BY SOUTHWEST

THE TAXI DRIVER

By Desiree Fischer

P arkway Station, you say?

That's gonna take a while, but I'll get you where you need to go. The whole motorway up north is blocked off. Someone decided to overturn their car. I hope you planned for extra time before your train.

Well, that was sensible of you. Might as well get comfortable. I got some peanuts on the dashboard. Won't be a penny extra, I promise. There are a couple of magazines in the door to your left if you fancy something to read. Nothing too saucy though, got a lot of families coming through here.

Ah, you're a journalist. So you're looking to transform the shit people tell you into gold? Well, it's going to cost a lot getting to the station in this traffic, so I might as well throw in something extra. Which nugget of gold can I offer you today?

What's my job like, huh? All of the questions in the world and you ask me that one. You people, all the same!

I often get asked what it's like to be a taxi driver. It's not because people are genuinely interested, it's only because they're obsessed with what everyone else is doing. Someone might do better, be more beautiful or happier. Because I'm polite I just give them the short answer. Something like, "It's different every day."

They don't expect, or want, any more than that. But since you're actually interested in the answer, I'll tell you. It really is different every single day.

I'm a friend, confessor, psychologist and doctor, all at the same time. No one would believe the things people tell me every single day. Things they'd never tell their family, or even their closest friend. But they can tell me, because I'm only a taxi driver. Our paths will never cross again and if they did, they can just ignore me. Or in case I want to talk, get a restraining order against me.

I'd never betray the secrets of anyone while I'm at work. Like priests and doctors. I feel what I'm told is confidential. What's been said in the taxi, stays in the taxi. I'm not even telling my wife. Even though sometimes she might guess; my beloved is a bit of a psychic.

But I'll tell you what, I find the people that don't talk when I'm driving, they're the ones that are the most interesting.

Why are they so self absorbed? What is it they don't even want to share with a taxi driver?

So I watch them. At every traffic light, every roundabout. Sometimes I even glance back when I'm driving. It's bad, I know, but you people interest me. The way your lives intertwine. The way you're so very blind when it comes to everything that's bloody obvious.

Please don't look at me that way. I know I shouldn't have sworn, I'm sorry.

So you're originally from London, eh? Chosen a lovely spot to live, if I may say so. I belong here; to this town, this beautiful stretch of land. Always been here, not looking to go anywhere else. I have to admit, though, I preferred it when there were more meadows and less of that industrial nonsense. Used to occupy a well back then. At least the pay is better now. The odd shilling chucked in here and there really didn't cut it, even back in those days.

Yeah, I know, I'm old.

You must be making decent cash as a journalist?

No?

I get it – Every day's the same and you're not getting anywhere, at least not where you dreamed you would be. You saw Pulitzers and cocktail parties in your future. You have ideas, lots of ideas, ones the Bristol Herald would never publish. Well, why don't you take them somewhere else then?

Yes, it's scary. New opportunities always are. If an old chap like me can learn to drive one of these metallic death traps, you can do what you actually want to do. What you dream of doing.

Sure, others might not be so forgiving of your mediocre style, but maybe that's what you need. All it takes is some effort and courage. Sadly nowadays both of these things are nothing more than words, drifting into the realms of the forgotten. And so will you, if you're not careful.

Before you know it the job you once loved and embraced will start to feel like cigarette smoke, you know what I mean? The faint shadow of excitement is still there, but so is the bitter aftertaste and that smell that will never really leave the room, or your life, for that matter.

You know what happens to people like you? They die. Yes, I know you all die. But at least most of you accomplish something, or try to, anyway. At least you love; at least you feel the pain of life. So what if the destination is shit? You might as well enjoy the ride, don't you think? You might as well love and laugh, cry and hate. Why not be brave and bold, instead of living a life full of mediocre days filled with average hours?

I know you find me interesting. But don't you think that instead of wallowing in chronic self-pity and looking jealously at everyone else's lives, you should live your own instead? Write what you need to write. The Bristol Herald is restructuring anyway. You're about to be sacked; applications for your job are already piling up on the editors' desk as we speak. It's all been signed off by HR days ago. Someone else can do it better and cheaper.

And spend some more time with the wife and the kids. She's thinking of divorcing you. The kids know your best mate better than they know you. And so does your wife, by the way, know what I mean?

If there's one thing I've learnt in my time here, it's that nothing can ever be as interesting as your own life. That's the only story you really need – write it.

I think this is where you need to get out.

ARKHANGELSK

elcome to the Noon Trai

ACL JUNCTION

THE NOON TRAIN

By Roz Clarke

R osa took her place in the queue for the turnstiles. The line shuffled towards the row of machines, glowing and gleaming in the dirty light of the station. During a moment's pause, Rosa considered one of the murals that were painted at intervals along the wide tunnel. NOVY ARKHANGELSK – ACL JUNCTION in retro-futuristic lettering, above an image of an industrial complex; a refinery or something of the sort, all black towers and steel domes. The station was underground, in tunnels beneath the northern biodome. They were many miles north of Novy Archangelsk, but there was nothing any closer worth mentioning. This region of Russia was a vast, industrialised plain interspersed with nominal wildlife sanctuaries. To Rosa, it was something like home. She'd grown up on a provincial rye farm; a few thousand hectares of heavily modified grass, grain destined for China. The local village dome was the modern equivalent of a family manor; nobody lived there who was not employed by Rosa's family business. Like any normal teenager, she had hated it, and left as soon as she could.

The farm no longer existed, of course. Oh, the fields of rye were still there, and the workforce was largely unchanged, but five months earlier Rosa's family had fled across the Bering Strait, anticipating trouble. More trouble. Worse trouble. Rosa had cursed them for cowards. Her mouth twisted now. They had seen the future with clearer eyes than she. They had described an unstoppable freight train thundering down Russia's track, and they had been proved right.

At the turnstiles, she waited and breathed carefully while the man in front of her stood beneath the arch of the metal detection portal. The light flicked from red to green and he stepped out the other side. Rosa walked forward; the light went red again. Although there was nothing that could give her away, she had to work to keep her heart rate even.

The triggering device was a spare external HUD attachment, and the software to control it was embedded in her own HUD. In her bag she carried a change of clothes, a small bottle of water and a vintage child's toy gun with a roll of equally antique, and far more important, gunpowder caps. She had a permit for the toy gun and a cover story about a cousin's daughter in Moscow with a birthday coming up. The girl and the birthday were real, and with luck Rosa would be handing the gun over in a few hours' time. She hoped her cousin would understand.

The machine matched the permit to the toy. The retinal scan beeped approvingly. Her implants being nothing out of the ordinary, the portal flicked to green, giving her leave to continue.

A spiral staircase with a lift running down its centre led up to a raised deck. Here, everything was glastic, and the refracted light from the sun, perched above the horizon, shot the walls through with pale gold. This stairway was the enchanted passage from the grim, cold November of Novy Arkhangelsk to the endless sunshine of the glittering mobile palace that constituted the first-class section of the Arctic Loopway. To the east she could see the more prosaic grey structure of the second and third class staircases, and beyond that the predatory shapes of the freight cranes, poised above the feeder tracks to either side of the main line. The rail line itself stretched to the horizon to east and west, raised on stanchions fifty metres above the tundra. She followed the signs to freight section

D, away from the shops selling imported American watches and Scottish shortbread.

Waiting in the freight section were containers carrying excess baggage, and others full of Russian fancy goods destined for Europe. Some of the wealthy passengers on this train would not be returning to the mother country; some of these containers probably held priceless art and family jewels. History repeated itself, thought Rosa, angry and sad and jubilant all at once. Her veins fizzed with adrenaline.

She found her container and flashed her code at the door's circuit. The mechanical bolt drew back, allowing the door to swing out under its own weight. She closed it behind her. There was one large trunk in the back of the container, and from it she drew a rugged laser cutter, a flexible softbox with a handle on each side, a tube of industrial glue, and a canister of something syrupy and dangerous. She cut a hole in the floor of the container, angling the cut and leaving one fine seam so that it would rest comfortably while the train was stationary. She was pleased with her plan, and soon she would get satisfaction.

She placed the laser cutter back in the trunk, spread glue on the cut segment of floor, and pressed the softbox to it. Two more minutes. She shook the last drops of water out of her bottle and packed the coil of caps into it, along with the spare HUD attachment, rewired to create a timed detonator. She pushed the HUD into the bottle, screwed the cap on, and dropped the bottle into the softbox. Using a plastic funnel, she poured the contents of the canister into the softbox. Her hands shook and her eyes and face stung from the vapours, but she managed to do it without spilling any of the deadly fluid.

She let out a long breath when the cap was tight on the softbox.

Shaking the tension out of her hands, she called up her HUD. She connected to the detonator, located the scheduled task that would arm the device and activated it. Time to go.

"Rosa!"

Oh hell. Through the sparkle of the menu on her HUD, dark against the bright rectangle of the container door, Rosa made out a familiar face. She held up a hand.

"Get out of here, Emile."

"You can't do this, Rosa! It's not the way. Stop it now and come with me. It's not too late."

"It is though." Rosa blinked the HUD closed. "It's armed." The adrenaline still coursed through her body, but the edge was fading.

She looked Emile in the eye. "You followed me?"

"I knew what you were planning. A tip-off."

"Really? Who else is in on this? Who else received this juicy titbit? Where's your bodyguard?"

He looked sad, and shook his head. "Nobody's in on it. There was nobody left I could tell. I sent Yvgeny away, somewhere safe. Carla has been arrested as a spy. They'll be coming for me next."

"Then why are you trying to stop me? You can see why this needs to happen. Denys has to die."

"And all the other passengers on the train? Everybody in the station? And the Loopway wrecked? This is foolish, Rosa. We need the Loopway. Besides, you're one of the few of us who doesn't have blood on their hands. It would be a good idea if you kept them clean."

She sank to her haunches and looked up at him. He looked worse than she felt. He let go of the handle of his suitcase and his skinny body sagged into the carbon fibre tubing of his exoskel, his arms drooping from his shoulders.

"Acceptable collateral."

"No. If you do this you'll wipe out our support at home *and* abroad."

"It's just the opposite, Emile. A message has to be sent. The world – what's left of it – needs to know what Denys has done, what the regime is planning. If I killed only Denys, do you think that would be the end of the Green Sickle? Of course not – one of his bully-boys would step into his shoes and carry on as usual. Normal service resumed, with scarcely a beat missed. I doubt they'd even interrupt the executions. No, Emile. No – dramatic measures are required."

"Have you so little faith in me, woman?"

She looked at him, and a rogue tendril of love pierced her heart. She dismissed it carelessly.

"I could regain my influence on the committee," he continued, "with Denys out of the way."

She laughed. "They'd kill you rather than bring you back into the fold. You know I'm right."

He looked hurt. She pushed back onto her feet and held out her hand. "Come on, let's get out of here."

"I can't let you do this. Please Rosa, if you love me, if you ever believed in the Sickle, disarm the bomb. We must rebuild together, and the Loopway is central – please, you must see how *stupid* this is."

"You insult me, but you are my brother forever, dear friend. I have to do this. What else can I do? Besides, I can't disarm it. There's no cancel command. I couldn't take any chances."

He blanched. He stretched his hand towards Rosa, and, from the arm-bone of his exoskel, extended his pistol.

Rosa was a fast draw – her hand went to her side quicker than thought – but she'd come unarmed. She might have smuggled something organic through the turnstiles; a blow-pipe or a bow, but she hadn't wanted to risk it. However things had soured behind the scenes, Emile was still one of the more recognisable faces of the revolution. He still had the respect, and fear, of most of the people of the New Union. They would not have looked too closely. The laser cutter was out of reach in the trunk, and in any case it would make a really lousy weapon.

"Then we take it with us," he said.

"Where would we take it? It's not like we can walk out through the turnstiles."

"This freight car. If we run it to the far end of the feeder line..."

She recovered her nerve. "I won't co-operate."

There was a clunk, a sensation of movement which quickly faded, and a persisting hum. "Too late. We're in the system. This car will be attached to the 11:00, no matter what we do. And now, thanks to you, we can't get out."

She stared blankly at the time on her HUD. 10:50. She had opted for a specific trigger time, rather than a countdown, not knowing exactly when she'd be able to arm the device. It was essential that it went off at noon precisely, when the train doors would be locked for departure. The Loopway trains were never late.

The container had a narrow band of glastic windows running along either side at eye level, and another bisecting it vertically. Beyond them, the lights in the pipe went from a flicker to a blur as they accelerated. A moment later and they were slowing down again. The car tipped to the right as the pipe curved to meet the Loopway, and halted.

Emile tugged at the door release.

"It's not going to open."

"No, of course not," he said.

They stared at each other for a long moment.

"How does it work?" asked Emile.

"What difference does it make?"

"Just tell me. Can we delay it?"

"No."

"Cut some wires somewhere? There must be something."

"No. The detonator is inside that box. Stick your fingers in that, they'll come back bone. The softbox is glued onto the section of floor underneath it, which I cut around so that when we start moving it'll be pulled out of the container by the low pressure, and into the Loopway. It's pretty fragile – it's designed to split when the noon train hits it – but it'll still work if it doesn't."

"How did you become so..." Words, apparently, failed him.

Rosa shrugged. "We fought for nine years to make things right, and – apologies for the cliché – but the cure has been worse than the disease. Denys mustn't get to the summit in Norway – I can't stand by and let Furey legitimise Denys' rule."

"Anne Furey can't legitimise anything. She's in a minority in her own government. The English won't do anything to provoke the US."

"What makes you so sure? The US is a spent force. The Chinese are ready to back Free Alaska; they invested so heavily in the Loopway, and they'd love to see an end to US influence over Arctic trade. Europe can't police the Norwegian Sea on their own, and we've already talked about strategic control of the Strait."

"She wouldn't talk to *us* about recognition."

"That was before Europe committed to backing the Norwegian tunnel."

"So that's why you targeted the Loopway."

"Yes. That's why."

The container moved again, and natural light pushed through the windows. The walls of the Loopway pipe were glastic from end to end – stronger and lighter than steel, it allowed the top-end tourists who rode the train just for the romance of it to see the landscape through which they hurtled. Then they were thrown forward and back as the magnetic couplings joined them to the 11:00. Both of them looked anxiously towards the softbox at the back of the container. It was intact, for the moment.

10:56. Four more minutes before departure, while the passengers debarked and embarked.

"Rosa, please help me here. At least let's try to buy a little time. We can talk it over, come up with a better plan. You know this is going to have the opposite effect to what you're aiming for, you must see that."

"There's no point, Emile. I told you, I can't stop it."

"So at the stroke of noon, a hundred people's deaths will be on your conscience."

"Don't try to pretend this is about protecting my innocence," she spat. "All you care about is the trade route."

Emile looked up at the little ovals of white sky visible through the windows. Suddenly, his gaze snapped back to Rosa.

"The HUD you used for the timer, that's a standard Steklo set?"

"Yes. So what?"

"Did you use a standard task? Referencing the system time?"

"Yes. But it doesn't matter, I can't fool it into a different system time, it's picking it up from the Loopway signal."

"Indeed, indeed; it's set to train time. That's the key!"

"What?"

"Twelve noon in the freight pipe at Novy Arkhangelsk is not the same thing as twelve noon on the Arctic Loopway. Oh, you are a resourceful woman, Rosa, but thank God you're not too br– you have your blind spots."

"What are you talking about?"

"If we stay on this train, we're in the clear for an hour anyway, correct? And as soon as we cross into the next time zone we go back in time and your clever little killing machine goes back too. We have the length of Russia to work something out."

Rosa began to argue that the train would be on NovArk time, but Emile wasn't listening. Keeping his pistol trained on her, he lowered himself to the floor of the container and eased his exoskel-assisted legs beneath either side of the softbox, taking its weight from the cut segment and holding it in place.

"No!" Rosa cried, and made to throw herself toward him.

"Don't be silly, *kishka*. I shoot you, or you split this bag and spill eat-your-flesh liquid all over my poor old legs. I don't much want either of those things to happen. Please stay still."

Rosa stayed still. She held her breath when 11:00 ticked over, and the train started to accelerate. She could see the pressure acting on Emile's legs, pressing the bottom of the softbox around them, but his exoskel was rigid, and easily held it in place.

"Well now," he said, almost cheerily. "I *am* in a fix. What is it, nitroglycerin?"

She shook her head. "Concentrated hydrogen peroxide, modified for viscosity."

"I won't ask where you got that from. I don't suppose it's too hard to come by. I wish you had talked to me before cooking up this plan."

Anger gripped Rosa. She dug her fingernails into her palms. She'd been through a lot to get this far; several sleepless nights and great risks taken. She wasn't doing it for vengeance, and yet she felt like Emile was robbing her of more than just a chance to kill Denys and make her point – he was robbing her of the *satisfaction* of killing Denys. And something more than that...

"Who do you think you are, Emile Liza? I recruited you into

the Sickle in the first place, I backed your stand for the Committee? You'd have been nobody without my help, so don't you sit there with your fancy fucking carbon fibre bone suit and tell me what I should or shouldn't have done!"

He held up his free hand in a gesture of peace, but the one with the pistol attached did not waver.

"It's not as if you had any better ideas. Denys has you running scared. You're a walking corpse and you know it!"

"You and I both, sister. I admit my plans need finessing. I was going to take the train East, go to the US and request asylum. With their backing, which I think I can reasonably expect, I can start to build a government in exile. Denys' coup is illegitimate, whereas we have the backing of the people. A referendum would support that. I have a ticket to Fairbanks and sympathisers waiting. Then I saw you at the station."

"And you couldn't just have left me alone?"

Emile looked out of the window. Some emotion flickered across his face that Rosa saw, but told herself she had not seen. She and Emile were comrades, and that was all.

"What were *you* going to do?"

Rosa took a deep breath and tried to shed the anger. "Ring the police and take responsibility. Go to Moscow and meet friends. Then the same as you, I suppose."

"You'd go into hiding – where? Belarus? Why not come with me to America?"

"Why *go*? If I was going to flee Russia I'd be on the *southbound* line. To China, to scour the refugee camps for my parents. No. I will make my way back to Moscow. We have support in Western Russia, more than you'd think. The people don't know the extent of Denys' crimes. Once they do, they will rally to our cause."

"Anything to make yourself relevant again, is that it? You think you can build an army?"

"I didn't say that," she said.

"But that's what you'll need. Denys has the generals in his pocket."

She sat cross-legged on the floor next to Emile. Outside, the sun still hung just to the left of zenith. It would move only fractionally before setting again. No, she reminded herself. Emile was right about that; they were moving around the Arctic Circle at the same speed as the Earth turned, give or take, against the direction of spin. The sun would hang right there, in the same spot just above the horizon, all the way around the Loop as far as the terminus at Mo i Rana. Few would see the whole trip through; it was a long shift even for the staff. In some ways she could see the romance of it, and it would certainly be nice to get more than a few paltry hours of daylight. She'd been based in Novy Arkhangelsk for several days, and in November it was dark for nineteen hours a day. But no, she would either be off the train in slightly over an hour, or dead in slightly less than one.

"I can deal with the generals," she said, but she wasn't as confident as she'd have liked.

"You'll be a terrorist," said Emile. "You'll be toxic to the movement."

"I don't think so." She steepled her hands under her chin as if in prayer; an unconscious gesture. "You know what this railway represents. The concentrated wealth of the oligarchs, the one per cent, the rich we had to eat, or be eaten by. Our constituency has been betrayed by Denys and the same old forces of cronyism and vested interests." In a bad American accent, she said softly: "This train don't carry nothin' *but* sinners. But, if that's how it turns out, if they manage to paint me as a terrorist, I can always fall honourably on my sword. I won't indict the rest of the moderates. Although that will be a lot harder to achieve with you here. Nobody will believe you weren't involved."

"That's true," said Emile. "You don't look as much like a villain as I do."

Sitting there with the white cube of the softbox in his lap, his face grey with stress and exhaustion, beads of sweat decorating his forehead despite the chilly air in the container, he did not look capable of villainy. Not even with the pistol trained on her. The exoskel was black and shiny with segmented plates over its joints, so it did have a vaguely insectoid appearance. At that moment, however, Emile looked like its helpless captive rather than its evil master.

She shook her head. "I can always put a bit more lipstick on, but you'd need a Darth Vader mask to look convincing."

He laughed, but he stopped laughing abruptly. "Don't do that," he whispered. He was looking at the softbox.

"It's fragile," said Rosa, "but not that fragile. Don't stress it at the corners, don't squeeze it hard, don't come near it with anything sharp."

"I have no intention of moving," he said. "At least in the short term. Sooner or later, though, we have to come up with some ideas."

"There is no 'we', Emile."

"What we need to do first," said Emile, as though she hadn't spoken, "is let the Loopway know about the bomb. They can stop this train, and the noon train. And the eastbound pipe had better be closed too, I suppose. They can get us out."

"You've got to be joking. They'd execute us both."

"So you're willing to kill for the cause, but not to die for it?"

"You make me sound like a monster," said Rosa. "I'm hardly the first person in history to – listen, I'm a soldier, not a martyr. It's my duty to kill for what I believe in, if there's no other way."

"Sound like a monster, or *feel* like one? Soldiers don't target civilians."

"Since when?" Rosa laughed unpleasantly. "You know, if I felt like we both ought to die – if I was ready for that – you know what I'd do?"

"I suppose," said Emile, "you would leap across this container, burst this softbox, let the explosive melt my legs off, probably melt half of your body too, drop through the floor, deliver your payload and blow up the noon train. It won't be as effective a demonstration as it would have been at NovArk, but better than nothing, right?"

"Right."

Rosa didn't move. Emile returned to staring over her shoulder, out of the window. She mirrored him in silence. The ground far below was a haze of dull yellow and dull purple, flecked with patches of thin snow and ice. The predicted snowstorm was taking its time in coming. Nothing moved out there. At this distance, at this speed, they wouldn't see anything small, and there was nothing large to see, outside of the few shale gas operations. There wasn't so much wildlife up here any more, outside of the central Arctic park. Hares, foxes, other little things that foxes ate. There were no trees, and in November no flowers. Nothing much to tug at the heartstrings, and yet Rosa was always moved by its bleak beauty.

"Going back to the problem of the generals," said Emile, "If you're putting your faith in your aunt, you are chasing unicorns, you know that. She won't back you this time."

Rosa kept her gaze fixed on the horizon, on the spot below the sun; the brightest place it was possible to look at directly. The sky was a vast bowl, white china tinged delicately with pink and blue. She felt she could almost see the curvature of the Earth. It was *easy* to imagine unicorns in such a place. Not mundane white goat-horses, but cloud-creatures, galloping down the slash of blinding light between the sun and the dark plains of the Province. Braided silver rivers carried the light through the tundra, snaking along the flat ground, joining, parting. Their speed was tremendous, yet smooth as satin. She felt that she, too, could be a sleek-sided unicorn flying through the sub-Arctic air.

"If she was going to take your side," Emile went on, "she'd have spoken out when they executed Kozlov."

It was Kozlov's murder that had sent her family packing. Rosa had failed to sway the Committee when it came to sovietising the new industries of the north; her background in farming was well known. She hadn't argued against the move, only against the summary execution of anyone putting up resistance. It had been made clear to her that there would be no debate, no consideration, no gentle transition from the old ways to the new. Rosa knew her history, but rational arguments based on well-documented past events fell on ears deafened by the roar of blood. It wouldn't have been so bad if their principles had held, but already it was obvious that new oligarchs would rise up and be stronger, more sharp-toothed than ever, having feasted on the bones of their predecessors.

It was getting stuffy in the container, though it was still chilly. Rosa considered the cold, fresh air outside the Loopway. The glastic tube was invisible apart from a dark flash on her retinas every second or so, where they passed a joint in the huge structure. It was solid, though, and it not only kept them safe in their high-speed, low-pressure bubble; it kept the world outside insulated from their passage. The air immediately around the train was a maelstrom of violent force, but she could not feel it, and outside the tube the wild world was undisturbed by their high-speed invasion. A cloud-unicorn could choose how much air it moved, Rosa supposed. She imagined a cool breath on her skin, as she swooped joyfully and inexorably around the planet. The faintest touch of warmth on her right cheek: the kiss of the motionless winter sun.

Emile's words sounded like they were coming from another place, another plane of existence.

"We'll cross the zone boundary with five minutes to spare. I never thought I'd be glad of that redraw in '15, never mind owe my life to it."

Reluctantly, she dragged herself back into her body, into the container, and looked at Emile. He had the thousand-yard stare of a man reading his HUD.

"It's going to be the same all the way round – cutting it fine, but crossing the boundaries just before each hour is up. It'll be like going back in time. If I were a little more comfortable, it would be quite exciting."

"I expect they're having a fabulous time in the passenger cabins. Chandeliers and champagne all the way."

"And caviar," said Emile.

"Yuck."

"Beats mealy worm burgers and rye porridge."

"Well of course it does," said Rosa, "but we didn't go through all this so that some people could wear tiaras and eat caviar on a fucking train like it's 1929!"

She was angry again, but the lines around Emile's mouth were getting deeper and that tendril of tenderness betrayed her once more.

"You're hungry?" she asked.

"Thirsty too, and I'm going to have to make a puddle pretty soon. I wasn't expecting this."

"Let the bomb go meet the noon train, and you can piss out of the hole in the floor."

"I doubt that," said Emile. "Haven't you ever tried to throw something out of a car window? That effect will be far stronger in this oversized tube. Didn't you read up on aerodynamics when you designed this thing?"

"I didn't design it. Well, not on my own. I came up with the basic concept and ran it through my contacts in – never mind, you don't need to know who. They specified the softbox." She shrugged. "I guess it's meant to keep the explosive contained until it's safely away from the train. *This* train."

"Well, that's interesting *kishka*, but it's academic. I'm not going to release the box."

"I haven't got anything to eat."

"We were supposed to be up there in the caviar cars. I haven't got much either but you can share these with me."

He pulled half a packet of chewy sweets from his pocket. Neither his eyes nor his pistol left Rosa. He tossed the sweets over to her.

"Unwrap one for me, can you?"

She did, and the two of them chewed in silence for a while. The sweets were cherry flavoured; plasticky but good. They ate them all, splitting the last one in half to share.

"I should hate you for this," said Emile. "I'm missing out on the best meals I would have had in weeks."

"I should hate you, too," said Rosa. "You're really screwing up my day."

"I think I've got it rather worse," said Emile. Although there was no sign on the dark fabric of his suit trousers, she could see urine pooling beneath his legs.

"Not for long, probably."

He shifted uncomfortably, and grimaced. "You'd think the little things wouldn't matter so much when you're staring death in the face. Or sitting with it in your lap. It's funny how they do."

"They don't if your blood's up. I fought on the front lines a few times during the revolution – back when they were still calling them riots, but they were running battles, really."

"I haven't forgotten, Rosa."

"You stop noticing your body altogether. I came out of those fights covered in cuts and bruises – a broken arm once. Baton strike. God, that hurt. But not until afterwards."

What she didn't say: *I was one of the lucky ones.*

"We'd never have won the revolution like that, you know?"

"That doesn't mean it was futile."

They subsided into silence again. It had been, Rosa thought, much worse than futile.

She stood up and stretched, feeling slightly guilty – Emile could not ease *his* cramps – and walked to the north-facing windows, away from the sun and towards the pole. She pressed her forehead against the glastic and tried to will herself into the form of a unicorn once more. Soon, they would cross the time zone boundary. If the device was reading railway time – NovArk time – there would be no change, and a few minutes after that it would blow. If it was reading local time, then it would be as Emile had said. Like going back in time. It wouldn't be the first occasion on which Rosa had changed time zones, but she'd never really felt what it meant before. Never been able, or perhaps never tried, to visualise the world spinning in space, herself drawing a tiny line upon it; direction of travel, meridians, latitudes. Time became concrete and substantial; the fourth dimension. She marvelled at the simple perfection of the universe. It pained her that, drawn upon the pristine mathematical reality of time, were these constructed, clumsy, human compromises.

The train hurtled along its gleaming, crystalline tube.

"Even the things we do best are ridiculous," Rosa murmured.

She didn't turn on her HUD. She kept her face pressed to the container's window until the surface grew warm and foggy. When she felt the subtle shift in pressures that indicated the train was braking, a burning tension flowed down through the muscles of her neck and back into her arms and legs, leaving them shaking and weak. She sat down again.

"We're not dead," said Emile. "How do you feel about that?"

"Like I wish I had something to throw at you."

"Well, I'm not sure how I feel either. One the one hand it's a relief, on the other hand it would be a relief to have it over with. Of course what would be best would be a change of trousers." He looked longingly at his suitcase.

"I'm sorry, Emile. Just for the trouser situation, mind you. Nothing else. You got yourself into this when you followed me."

When the train halted at Novy Urengoy, Emile said, "So, what now? If you want to get off I won't stop you. I'll call for help, of course, but I'll keep your name out of it. I can say I found the device like this and nobody with it. Perhaps they won't execute me."

She waved at the still-visible landscape outside the windows.

"This container is booked to go to Usinsk. We are both going to Usinsk whether we like it or not."

Between Novy Urengoy and Usinsk the train passed through six more time zones. Rosa grew faint with thirst, hunger and the relentless threat of Emile's pistol. Then she grew numb, and eventually she slept a little. As far as she could tell, Emile did not close his eyes at all. In any case, she didn't know how sophisticated the software that controlled his exoskel was. It was quite possible that his HUD could track and shoot her while he dozed.

"I can't believe you're still sitting there," she said to him, around forty-five minutes out from Usinsk. The air had grown foul, but the light in the container had not changed since their departure from Novy Arkhangelsk, and nor had the tundra beneath the magnificent railway line. A casual observer would note few differences between the scene now and that of six hours previously. Only the faces of the two protagonists reflected the passage of time.

Emile's response was slow and strained. "I have no more desire to be executed than you do. Or to see *you* executed, sweet rose. Are you willing to talk plans yet?"

"My head hurts."

"My everything hurts. Let's figure our way out of this. You want to kill Denys; I can support that. And you want to damage this gleaming symbol of inequality; that is understandable but it's also an intolerable waste. It took years of international co-operation, brings untold economic benefits and is beloved by millions. It is built and cannot be *un*built. What we need to do is turn it to the benefit of the people."

"Like all the other things we thought we'd be able to turn to the benefit of the people? Listen to yourself, Emile. Try to remember everything that's happened in the past twelve months. Your idealism is *very* sweet but you sound like you haven't learned a bloody thing. And I know that's not the case. Why would the train be any different to the gas fields, or the factories, or the farms? Or the submarines, or the TV stations? Or the internet? Every single fucking thing we thought would empower the ordinary people has been taken and twisted and used to control and exploit them."

"How do you hope to rebuild based on such cynicism? What are you going back to Moscow to do?"

"Stop the killing. Just – make it stop." She counted ragged breaths until she felt her pulse subside, then went on: "If we take it slowly we can patch things up, get the justice system back on track, and the bureaucracy. Then we can talk about what kind of society we want to live in. Start again. Have that conversation with the people of the Union, over again, and this time we'll listen. We were so caught up in what *we* thought was right..."

"Don't you see the contradiction? You preach gradual change, but you're utilising your enemies' tactics. This – blowing up the train, slaughtering people instead of applying due process – this is exactly what they've been doing. Exactly what you've been fighting against. Let them carry on and sooner or later the tide will turn against them. We can ride that tide home."

"No, Emile. They *wouldn't* blow up the train. They would execute the current owners of the line, seize it, and 'redistribute' it straight into the pockets of their backers. The only reason they haven't done that already is the Chinese interest."

"I can hardly believe I'm having to say this, Rosa, but you can't usher in a new era of hope if you start out by slaughtering civilians and wrecking essential infrastructure!"

His raised voice brought Rosa's pulse to a racing frenzy once more.

"If I can't, neither can you!" she yelled. She turned away and pressed her hands against the curved container wall. When she turned back, his head hung down over the softbox. She couldn't hear him breathing. Worried he'd passed out, she rushed to his side and lifted his chin. Tears ran down his cheeks.

"Look at me, Emile. Are you all right? Look at me!"

He took a deep, shuddering breath, then another. His eyes tight shut, he tried to twist his head away from her. His mouth opened and closed, opened and closed, just as her friend Sofia's had done when the bullet ripped her lung open, and she toppled from the barricade into the street. She had lain with her head in Rosa's lap, and died. The look in her eyes said *make this worthwhile*. Rosa had vowed that she would.

She tried to prise Emile's eye open with her thumb and forefinger, to force him to look at her. He would not. She let go of him and fell to the floor.

She didn't know what had snapped inside Emile, but his refusal to look her in the eye was worse than any of his rhetoric. A tear – just one, barely a tear at all – moistened her own cheek. She lay waiting for him to relent, and when he didn't, she shuffled around behind him, and put her arms around his waist. She had to wriggle her hands between his body and the softbox. The damp patch around him had almost dried, but there was still a sour smell. Inside the exoskel and under his decent suit he was thin and soft. She rested her head against his back, alongside the ridge of the exoskel's spine. His pistol arm reached around his body in a vain effort to keep a lock on her. She chuckled softly.

"I can't feel my feet," he whispered.

"The weight?"

"Yes. Help me, Rosa. I'll help you."

She thought for a moment. Drifts of snow and silver clouds filled her closed eyes. She realised dimly that she wasn't thinking at all; she was past thought.

"All right."

There was no sense of revelation, nor acceptance, nor of giving in, nor anything breaking. No obvious turning point was reached.

She had no sense of anything apart from the feel of Emile's serge suit fabric against her face and the vibration of the train beneath her thighs. The complex smell of his humanity. The train rushed onward, the world spun around, and the sun hung still in the sky.

Without urgency, she broke her own reverie. The connection between the two of them seemed to survive their physical separation, even though Emile's eyes remained closed. She stroked his hair and leaned his head back against the frame of the exoskel. She gently lifted one eyelid; he was unconscious, or very deeply asleep. She looked at his frail body, seeking out places she could rub his blood back into motion. The exoskel made it difficult enough, not to mention the deadly softbox, but she did what she could.

Without wondering why she was doing it, she considered the softbox. She could only see one thing she could use to replace Emile's legs as a prop; the laser cutter. Making doubly sure that the safety was on, she started to work the tool under Emile's leg. His dead weight, the rigid exoskel and the rolling weight of the softbox all worked against her. It took a while, but she finally forced the cutter into place. Emile would have bruises to show for it.

She couldn't move him yet though – only one side of the box would be supported, and it could still easily slip through the hole in the container. What else could she use? The total contents of the container were her overnight bag – her knickers were unlikely to be any help – Emile's suitcase, the cutter, the softbox and the two humans. Emile's suitcase was the kind with wheels on one end and an extending handle. The handle was already extended. It looked flimsy, but when she tried to bend it with her hands, it held.

It proved much easier to slide the suitcase handle under Emile's leg than the bulky cutter had been. She still didn't like the look of the skinny tubes of metal, but she took a deep breath, put her arms under Emile's shoulders and dragged him backwards.

It took an eternity of tiny shifts: drag, adjust the legs, adjust the props, drag some more. Centimetres at a time, she eased her comrade out from underneath the softbox. Belatedly, she realised the hard edges of the cutter and the handle could pose a threat to the skin of the box, and she pulled a couple of shirts out of Emile's case and used them to cushion it.

When Emile was free at last, she hugged him, ignoring the pistol that the exoskel still insisted on shoving into her chest. She wished she could lie him down, but she wasn't strong enough to overcome his servo-motors, and much as she despised the skel at that moment, she didn't want to damage it. She'd never known Emile without it; whatever had happened to him had been before they'd met, when they were both students in NovArk. Back when the Green Sickle was an environmental protest group. Perhaps he'd been born needing it. It wasn't something he talked about.

She looked anxiously at the box. It was definitely reacting to the stresses of the air around the train. She hadn't promised not to let the bomb go, just to help Emile. She'd done that; he was safely away from the box. His pulse was steady when she checked it. She could take the props back out and let it fall. Let the train race on away from that point, carrying her and Emile to their new lives. Let the device meet its appointment with the noon train. She could see it in her mind's eye; the explosion, the Loopway cracking, the fireball engulfing Denys. Other people too, but they were almost faceless. In her imagination they wore evening dress and dripped with diamonds, and laughed as they shovelled forkfuls of caviar into their fat-lipped mouths. They had no eyes, no souls. Denys hadn't killed Sofia, but he had betrayed her; he had betrayed everyone who had died for the Sickle. He had betrayed the green movement, betrayed the social revolution. He had betrayed the future as well as the past. The earth was not safe in the hands of men like him; nothing was. He *did* deserve to die; she had no doubt whatsoever about that. Her anger ran so deep it made her want to vomit.

And yet the plan that made sense that morning in NovArk did not fit together in her brain any more. When she tried to imagine the future, she saw only the golden double-line of the Loopway stretching from horizon to horizon across the warming tundra and around the Arctic Circle like a halo. Herself, riding it like a figurehead, a snow-cloud woman with silver hooves and a single crystal horn in the centre of her forehead.

The flexing of the softbox decided her. Immediate problems could be solved immediately; she was in no fit state for the big ones. She used Emile's remaining clothes and her own – knickers coming in handy after all – to fashion a rope which she strung between the handle of the softbox and the hatch-lock bar of the container. If that didn't hold, well, there was nothing else she could do.

A few sharp flicks on his cheek with her fingernail, and Emile fluttered back to consciousness as the train started to brake for Usinsk.

"What time is it?" he rasped.

"Sometime between eleven and twelve, same as it has been all day, idiot."

"Care to be... more specific?"

"Definitely not."

She saw him take in the makeshift rope and the re-propped softbox before checking his HUD, but he didn't say anything.

"This container will be detached here?" asked Emile, blinking hard.

"Yes. About five minutes after we stop, if it's the same procedure."

"Then what?"

"Same as when we got on. Shuttled down one of the feeder lines and into a collection point."

"Which took... about ten minutes?"

"There's no guarantee it will be the same, but more or less."

"It's long enough. We get down there and get out-"

"No."

"What do you mean, 'no'?"

"It *might* be long enough, but that's not the plan."

He groaned. "I hate your plans."

She pointed at the softbox.

"That thing is glued to the cut section of the container floor. Together, they're heavy."

"I know, thanks."

"Too heavy for me to lift out. But not for you?"

His eyes lost focus for a second before he nodded. "I'm a bit low on power, but I think it'll be within specs."

"I've propped one side up on my laser cutter. Can you hold it in place again if I take the cutter out?"

"Why?"

"I'll use the cutter to open the hatch."

"You're aiming to leave the bomb in the container?"

The look on Emile's face threw her.

"Well…"

"Hellfire, Rosa. Tell me that's not the plan? You know I won't let you do it. I'm the one with the gun, remember."

She thought of the toy gun in her bag and fervently longed for a real one. "What are we going to do, stay on the train and keep going round the Loopway until tomorrow? It's going to go off eventually."

"Until tomorrow." He looked thoughtful. "It would be good to have a tomorrow. Together."

She threw up her hands. "What are you on about?"

"You said it yourself. You love me."

"Don't be an *idiot*."

Then she had an idea. The toy gun was a pretty good imitation. Emile was no firearms expert. She inched across to her bag, reached inside it and drew the thing. After all this time, Emile's guard was down; he wasn't even looking at her. She aimed it at him; it had to be worth a try.

"We seem to have a stand-off."

He rolled his eyes and for a moment she thought her ruse had failed.

"You think you can fire quicker than my software?"

"I'm willing to see if I can."

"Fine. Your plan. But not because of the gun, all right? I just can't bear another fifteen minutes in this container."

Rosa smiled.

#

"You feel that?"

"We've stopped. OK, go."

"We're just delaying the inevitable," Rosa said as they wrestled the box, cut container floor and all, into Emile's suitcase. On the fullest expansion it barely fitted, and zipping the case closed was a terrifying experience. There was no space to pad it. "You should have let me drop it out of the train."

"Maybe not even delaying," admitted Emile. "One knock and we're sky-high. This is a very risky plan, Rosa. I don't think much of it. *You* really should have woken me up."

She snorted.

Outside the hatch they found a narrow service platform. Rosa let out a relieved breath. "I wasn't a hundred percent sure there'd be a platform here. We'd have been stuck if there was nothing but Loopway tube."

"Now you tell me," said Emile.

"That way." Rosa pointed to a small door at the eastern end of the platform. "It must link this section to the passenger platforms."

"Let's hope so," said Emile. "I can't get station schematics; they're security classified."

The door was locked, but Rosa had brought the laser cutter and they were through in short order.

She jogged down the corridor on the other side of the door, ahead of Emile, who clanked steadily along, dragging the bulky suitcase. Another locked door and they were suddenly on a platform thronged with Loopway passengers, standard class. These people were well-to-do, the top 20% perhaps, but not the super-rich that would be riding in first class. Rosa looked at them; expectant holiday faces and jaded commuter faces, elderly people, children and young lovers, and surprised herself by hoping they didn't have to die that day.

A tannoy counted down the time to departure. She kept one hand on Emile's elbow until the crowd boarded the train, then ushered him towards the nearest door. They re-embarked with seconds to spare, hauling the case into the vestibule after them; an exercise in the balance of speed and caution.

She hugged him again, and they both laughed, giddy with exhaustion and delicious oxygen.

"I think I'm going to throw up," said Emile, and left Rosa guarding the case while he staggered into the toilet.

"You forgot these," she told him when he returned, and thrust her overnight bag at him, which now contained a change of pants and trousers for him. She'd made time to retrieve them. Of all the things she'd done that day, subjecting him to that humiliation was the one she felt worst about.

He went and changed, and then she took her turn to freshen up.

"It's not usually this way round, is it," she remarked to Emile, back in the vestibule. By now the train was well underway again. The doors had large panes of glastic, affording them a dazzling panoramic view. Storm clouds gathered, but their bulk rested above the lantern sun, only making it seem brighter.

"What?"

"Usually the hero and heroine start off dressed to kill, then end up trapped and in danger and all scuffed up. Things are looking up for us."

"I suppose they are," he said, "At least I'm not so thirsty any more – I know the tap water on the trains is recycled and grim; you tried it? Nothing ever tasted so good to me. And the clean underwear is heavenly. But now what? My seat's all the way up in first class, you haven't got a ticket, and we're still babysitting a bag of explosive."

"It had hardly slipped my mind."

"We can't walk this thing up the train."

"Too risky." She shook her head. "You need something to eat?"

She squeezed his arm as he nodded, hurting her hand on the rigid exoskel.

"You go. Tell the train manager you got confused at NovArk or something, and got onto the wrong train."

"NovArk was hours and hours ago. That's not going to fly."

"You'll think of something."

"I don't know. My brain feels like it's been scooped out, mashed and piped back in through my ear."

"Go anyway. There's no point both of us staying here. They can't arrest you for being on the wrong train."

That was when she kissed him. There was something about the moment of betrayal that unlocked her compassion. Perhaps believing that she would never see him again unlocked her love.

Startled, he returned the kiss. It was not a deft, cinematic kind of kiss; it was awkward and she broke off, laughing again. He laughed too. His hands on her waist, he looked into her eyes.

"Give me the laser cutter."

His pistol-arm was jammed into her ribs. "Damn you. *Damn* you." She handed it over. "I suppose you want the gun too?"

"Not really," he said. "You can't do too much damage with that."

"If you want to save everyone so damn much," said Rosa, full of fury, "get the detonator out of the box. One arm, for all these lives and your precious railway line. If you're going to be a bloody hero it's not much of a price, is it?"

"If I could be sure I'd survive the experience, I might, but no thanks. The Union needs me."

She rolled her eyes. Together, they manoeuvred the case into the bathroom cubicle, and Rosa locked herself in. She wedged the case between two walls and the toilet pedestal, and, regretting the stench, sat down where her body formed a fourth barrier, keeping the case from moving. Her stomach growled; it was suppertime in Novy Arkhangelsk. It would have been dark for many hours. She was surprised to find she longed for darkness. There was no window in the bathroom, but she knew precisely where the sun was, precisely what the shadows of the Loopway stanchions were doing. The suspension of hours that had seemed mathematically divine a few hours before now felt like an oppressive limbo. She tried to put herself back into that trance-like state, but there was a knot of nausea and disappointment lodged in her gut where her last meal should have been. She traced a line on the wall where she'd have cut through it, if she'd been able. She dozed off, and dreamed of being chased around a carousel by a fire-breathing lion.

She woke up. The vibration of the train's movement was missing. They had stopped, which could mean only one thing – Arkhangelsk ACL. Emile wasn't there. He hadn't come back. Her heart skipped a beat. She struggled to her feet and palmed the bathroom door open. On the other side of the vestibule, the door to the platform was open, and an old woman was boarding the train. Rosa heard the tannoy announcement: twenty seconds to doors locked, thirty seconds to departure. Where was Emile? A sensible thought poked its nose up amongst the muddle of her panic. She checked her HUD and there it was; a message from Emile. He was stuck in first class – why? – and she was to get off at AACL. *Damn.* There was no time to question it. She pulled the case out of the bathroom behind her, almost roughly, and swore at herself, startling the old lady. She glared at the woman, willing her to move faster, and the woman glared back. The case was so heavy it was a struggle to get it through the train door, and the warning beep was sounding before she was through. If the door closed on the case it was all over. Rosa broke a sweat. Then she and the case were somehow safely on the platform.

She regarded the train in desperation. The countdown completed, the doors closed. She heard the final hiss and clunk of the seals closing. The chase would continue, but the trains; this one and the noon train; were just modes of transport now. No cloud unicorns. No lions of fire. Bereft, Rosa let out a whole string of curses. She was busy colouring the air blue when a pair of scrawny arms reached around her and held her close.

"Where the hell were you? What happened to going to Norway? Why the fuck did I get off the train, just because you *told* me to? I'm so *stupid*."

"I'm sorry, Rosa. We can't cross the border. Not on the train. I ran into Maitland. Come here."

He took hold of the case and pulled her towards a service door like the one they'd used at Usinsk.

"Maitland Shesh? The Canuck fink?"

"Sure, if you like. He's our fink too, but never mind that. He *knew*, Rosa. He knew what you were planning. I heard him talking to someone – in English – he knew there was going to be an assassination attempt on Denys. He's been on the train since NovArk too, and he's been up and down it looking for you."

"But he didn't find me."

"You didn't hear the announcement about possible delays before the border crossing? They're blaming it on storms, but -"

"You had the cutter," she interrupted him.

"Oh. Hm. I left it on the train."

He looked down the platform. Uniformed men and women appeared at the exits, conspicuously armed and agitated.

Luckily for them, and unluckily for her, a station worker chose that moment to come through the service door. Rosa levelled her fake pistol and told her to open the door and let them through. She tried to refuse, but then she recognised Emile, and wordlessly led them into the corridor and onto the platform by the points section where the freight cars waited.

"What are you doing here? Where are you going?" she asked.

"Away from here, as fast as possible. Can we get to the border in thirty minutes?"

Rosa checked her HUD. Just gone eleven. Thirty minutes to the docks and then – what? Thirty more minutes to go – where? Only a tiny part of her mind was focussed on these questions. It was as

though her brain had been reduced to a problem-solving subroutine
– a poor one, in a cold shell – while her soul, her glowing, galloping,
purposeful self, had left aboard the train.

The station worker shook her head.

"We won't hurt you, but you have to help us. Otherwise a lot of
people here, at the station, could get hurt. OK?"

The worker swallowed hard and held up one hand, quieting him
while she checked something on her HUD. After a few long, painful
seconds, she shook her head again.

"None of these for the border, today. Arkhangelsk, Moscow."

"You don't understand," said Emile, "This case contains-"

"I understand perfectly," whispered the woman. "They paged us
all about the... about you people."

"What are you doing?" Rosa asked Emile. In the detached way
that was all her empty shell was capable of, she realised she had
completely lost control of the situation. However, she suspected
Emile was no more in control than she was, even if he had an actual
weapon and she didn't.

Emile ran his hands through his hair, tugging at the roots. His
eyes looked bruised.

"Is there somewhere we can hide?"

Rosa turned on him. "Hide? What good would that do?"

While the two of them were focussed on one another, the station
worker turned on her heels and made to flee. Without hesitation,
Emile shot her in the leg. She screamed and fell sobbing to the
ground.

"OK," said Rosa. "That *was* pretty fast."

She took the woman's pager out of her pocket and handed it to
Emile, and then bound her wound. The bullet had taken a slice out
of her muscle but it hadn't hit the bone. It was clinically done.

Emile apologised. "They will kill us if they find us," he explained. The woman just stared at him in round-eyed agony.

"How can we avoid the police?" he asked.

The freight containers behind them hummed and disappeared down the tunnel.

"Tell me." Emile jabbed his pistol wrist towards the worker.

"She's not going to tell us anything," said Rosa. "Hang on a moment."

She went back into the service corridor, propping the door ajar with her bag. She tensed, expecting at any moment the door to the platform would be opened by the hunters pursuing her, but she reached the point she was looking for without that happening. A ladder stretched up and down though a narrow space, and it was – yes! – it was curved to wrap around the Loopway.

She went back for Emile. They left the wounded woman where she was; it wouldn't take long for someone to find her.

It was fiercely cold on this side of the door. From below, Rosa heard the wind whistling around the Loopway. Emile said he didn't like the look of the ladder, but Rosa urged him onwards. He went first, taking the weight of the case, and Rosa guided it down into his waiting arms. He wobbled as he took hold of it, and Rosa bit back a scream. If they dropped it, they would die. It looked so innocuous, so *luggage*-like, but the insane weight of it was an effective reminder.

When they passed beneath the level of the station's structures and approached the underside of the pipe, the walls disappeared, leaving only an open latticework of cream-painted steel between her and a heart-stopping fifty-metre drop. The wind whipped her hair into her face and stole the air from her lungs. She froze, and Emile called to her.

"What's the matter?"

"Can't we just stay here until they've gone?"

"This was your idea, woman! And if I can remind you, everything that's happened today has been your idea, so you damn well keep moving – unless you want to die here? I'm just as scared as you are and *I'm* not stopping."

"You're not as scared as I am then, are you?"

Slowly, deliberately, he shifted himself and the explosive suitcase along another rung.

"All *right!*" she shouted, but for a long moment she couldn't move. She had to tell each finger individually to release the rung she was holding. Finally she managed it. Below the centre of the double pipe the ladder met another, running lengthwise. Emile shifted the case to behind him and came along backwards, saying it was easier. Not looking down, they traversed the ladder. As they clambered, they talked, shouting to make themselves heard over the wind. They talked until they were hoarse; about the good old days, when the Green Sickle glittered with ideas and ideals, and they were young, and drunk on black market vodka, hope, and their own cleverness. In love with their own passion. They talked about the months when the streets had burned and the glorious day when the tanks stopped rolling towards the protesters, and rolled towards the Kremlin instead. They talked about the machinations after power had been claimed, and the Sickle soaked in blood and death and disappointment. They talked about Denys. They made a plan, together.

When they came out of the shadow of the station, the ladder again formed a T, the arms reaching up and around the pipe. Emile turned right and began to climb up. Rosa stopped to catch her breath, pressing her forehead into the cold steel rungs. It had taken an eternity. She flashed the time up on her HUD. A quarter to noon

– this escapade had taken almost all the time they had left. There was only going to be one outcome, after all.

She clung to the structure with the last of her strength as the noon train hummed into the station.

"Rosa," said Emile. "I'm almost out of power. I'm down to three percent."

"I know just how you feel." Her own limbs were leaden and trembling.

The ladder brought them out into another service corridor, at the eastern end of the first-class platform. This time the only exit was in that direction, where the train waited and the passengers came and went. They waited behind the door, one with an arm that functioned as a gun and one with a gun that functioned as nothing, until two minutes to twelve. Emile had to shoot his way through the door, which attracted some alarmed attention. The guards were still there, but the crowds stopped them from reaching Emile and Rosa before they could get on the train. Emile lifted the case smoothly aboard, and Rosa came behind, keeping the other passengers clear of it.

As soon as they were in the vestibule – markedly more plush than the standard-class one, with brass fittings and velvet curtains – Emile pushed her in front of him into the corridor. To their left was the platform, police visible through the large windows, pushing their way towards the train. To their right were doorways leading into private cabins; clever sleeping, dining and working spaces for the most elite passengers. Outside one door, halfway down the carriage, stood two of Denys' bodyguards. Over Rosa's shoulder, Emile shot them both. In the head. They went down like bags of meat.

Rosa opened the cabin door and brandished her gun. She had thought of nothing smart to say, as she hadn't expected to ever actually see the man again. "It's over for you, Denys!" was the disappointing result.

The train hummed, preparing for departure. Emile went to pull the case into the cabin, but he stopped dead halfway through the doorway. His knees buckled, and he slumped to the floor.

Rosa realised what had happened before Denys could react. His power had run down. She hurled her exhausted body across the carriage and rammed her toy pistol into Denys' throat, where he wouldn't be able to see it. It felt cold and hard in her hand, and that gave her courage.

Denys wasn't dumb enough to ask what they were doing there. Instead, he said, "I knew we shouldn't have tried to marginalise you two; so resourceful. I had bad advice. Talk to me now. Any positions you want on the Committee, you can have."

Emile spoke up from the floor. "There's just one thing we need you to do, old chap, before we go any further. Otherwise we'll all be taking positions a hundred yards wide across the tundra."

Rosa pushed Denys across to the suitcase, keeping the muzzle of the pistol pressed to his flesh. She had her HUD up. 11:59:47. Since they'd disembarked the earlier train, the sun had resumed its arc across the sky, but she had not seen it. Time, now, and not the train, rushed headlong into eternity.

Rosa grinned, unzipped the suitcase and unscrewed the cap of the softbox, quick and deft; thrumming with adrenaline. Seven seconds. Her mouth centimetres from Denys' cheek, she said, "Just pop your hand in there, would you Denys, and fish out that water bottle?"

Maybe it was the slight sting of the fumes coming from the softbox, maybe it was just the context, but Denys' face changed colour and he cringed away. Rosa kept a firm hand on the back of his head, and jabbed his throat with the toy gun again. He leaned forward, and reached out a trembling hand.

Across his bent head, Rosa's eyes met Emile's and sparks flew between them. The power of the train's vast electromagnets transferred to her body, to her blood. She had been reunited with her soul, and it surged up in anticipation of the train's departure. It leaped like a racehorse longing to be out on the track, eating time and space with its flying hooves. The fire would catch in the very mouth of the lion, and perhaps, just perhaps, its jaws would contain it.

LIKE GIANTS

By Kevlin Henney

Like giants... we were like giants. It was when we walked... when we walked like giants... like giants across the earth, across the water, from land to sea to land to sea to rest at last. To rest on earth once more.

Like giants... were we? No... on giants. I remember now... I remember then... we were not giants, we were on giants, we rode them, rode them from the mountains... rode them into the sea, from the mountains in the north to the oceans of the south. We rode them across the sea by way of the glistering moon, upon its wavering beams, through night to dawn, to night once more, each moment, each day, ceding to the next. Night... day... night... day... storm clouds... clear skies... storms once more, one pattern of sky leapfrogging the next to make the journey, leapfrogging one another like giants.

We rode them, yes... but did they walk? Did the giants stride across landscape, across sea? Did they stride with purpose, stride to save us, carrying us away, carrying us to salvation? No... they too were swept, as we were, swept away... uprooted from earth, helpless, saving handfuls of us through fortune, fortune without resolve, without design, without heart.

We paid the price, the toll, to journey until dawn, through daybreak and beyond, away from the fall of night, away from the fall of water that broke upon our village, that took it all away... the cascade from the mountains in the north, washing all we had known into darkness, like spillage into night, the fall of a cauldron knocked from the fire... quenching the fire and embers and lives around it... the mothers, the fathers, the brothers, the sisters.

It was late, it was dark, most were asleep... the cascade from the north washed us further into darkness, like falling stars across the sky... like fallen leaves upon the ground, swept by rain, scattered by morning... scattered in mourning.

Washed away... away. Swept and scattered, we were.

We were like trees... they were like trees, a forest moving on waves. We rode upon them, we rode upon trees. We rested upon their shoulders, nested in their leaves, through broken valleys to the break of day, sheltered and skeltered. The trees were the giants that rode and rolled above and through the water, holding us above the flotsam and flow, of the villages and fields and forests taken by the water, pulled from their roots, torn from their homes. Swept away... away.

The cold deep hearts of the mountains had shed their skin of ice and tree. Like giants the flooding waters came from the north... came and stole us away, stole our lives, our homes... took us away, took us here... delivering us a new home.

We were from the north... so long ago... home has been here for so long, so far south, south across sea and land by sea that crossed the land, that rose to make shallows of islands in its path, taking us on, cradled in trees, nested in leaves.

Another time we would have laughed, from the joy that borders fear, thrilled to be swayed and tossed, taken by the waves across the land. Another time we would have held the hands of our mothers and fathers, held back from crossing the edge of fear, knowing all would be well... the hands of our brothers and sisters, knowing all would be together.

Another time.

This was not that time... not the time of our lives, but the time of death and holding onto life, a time of fear alone, fear without safety, fear without thrill. A race no one had chosen to run, a time without knowledge. Would we be together? Would there be a time that followed this time, a time from when we could look back? Look back like giants, to tower over this past, to stand over our loss... to stand in silence and then reclaim laughter.

Would there? Would we?

We were like giants chasing the day's end through sunset into moonrise, taken south by the current, west by the wind. Racing the sun but always losing, always overtaken on the other side of night. But better to chase the sun than have it hide. Night brought a stillness that sometimes held sleep, but more often a stillness to be uncalmed by memory or a storm that lashed us with waves and whipped us with fear, stealing calm... stealing souls... loved ones forgotten into the sea, discovered at daybreak, remembered with streams of tears, tributes to the ocean.

That sea of people swept from one village and the next and more, families and forests together, brothers and sisters holding onto trees, pushed above the waves by mothers and fathers... mothers and fathers like giants, offering strength and salvation... until strength failed and to save was to let go... the cries and the crying, the farewells lost in waves.

So few arrived here, so long ago.

Like giants... we were like giants. It was when we walked... when we walked like giants... like giants along the shore, down from the shoulders of our trees, delivered from the sea at sunset... after how many nights? After so many nights.

Children... we were children... children with long shadows, long shadows cast from grief and failing light. We had been brothers and sisters, but there were no brothers and sisters on that shore... and of the fewer who had been mothers and fathers, they were parents only to grief.

All that happened... all that there was before... no more than dream, half remembered, most forgotten. The turning flow of years has swept this past from us. New families forged from loss, forged from survival... families from families, born anew, new roots set down into the earth.

Into the earth.

And before I rest for the last time, this is my wish, my final wish for my place of rest. Into the earth and not the sea.

NORTH BRISTOL WRITERS

John Hawkes-Reed is a Unix hacker by day. By night, too, if it's been one of those sorts of weeks. His origin story involves finding the big yellow Gollancz hardbacks in Winchcome public library, the *Making a Transistor Radio* Ladybird book and the John Peel programme. The 2006 Viable Paradise writer's workshop was something of a life-changing experience, and he has been quietly emitting stories of varying length since then. Some of those stories can be found in the anthologies *Airship Shape and Bristol Fashion*, *Colinthology*, *Dark Spires* and *Future Bristol*. He is fascinated by cold-war architecture, islands and stationary engines. John owns too many books, not enough tractors and is trivially Googleable.

Jemma Milburn co-founded North Bristol Writers Group, after almost one wonderful year of steadily trying to keep it on the rails however, it was time to move to Cambridge for work. She is now settled down in The Fens and has taken very much a back seat now that the group has gained momentum. Jemma has always enjoyed frantically scribbling down words to create some kind of artistic outpouring in between her science work. It was only recently with the birth of NBCW that she decided it might be a good idea to give these 'pieces' some kind of direction, with the help of a group to attend. She also enjoys drama and collaborative theatre, which explains her approach to writing using tools such as characterization and an organic approach to story building.

Ian Millsted is a writer and teacher who lives in Bristol with his wife and daughter. His fiction has appeared in the likes of *Airship Shape and Bristol Fashion* and *Colinthology*. He has been shortlisted for the Bristol Short Story Prize. His non-fiction has appeared in *Back Issue* and the *Times Educational Supplement*. He's scripted comic strips for Comics International. Despite having migrated to Bristol some years ago he still supports Essex in cricket and West Ham in football.

Pete Sutton has a not so secret lair in the wilds of Fishponds, Bristol and dreams up stories, many of which are about magpies. He's had stuff published, online and in book form, and currently has a pile of words that one day may possibly be a novel. He wrote all about Fishponds for the *Naked Guide to Bristol* and has made more money from non-fiction than he has from fiction and wonders if that means the gods of publishing are trying to tell him something.

You can find him all over social media or worrying about events he's helped organise at the Bristol Festival of Literature. On Twitter he's @suttope and his Bristol Book Blog is here: http://brsbkblog.blogspot.co.uk/ He's contributing editor of *Far Horizons* e-magazine which can be found here: *http://info-far-horizons.wix.com/far-horizons-emag*

Clare Dornan now lives in Montpelier having spent the last 20 years in Bristol.

Her day job is making documentaries for television about science, wildlife and madcap expeditions in far flung places. She studied zoology at Cambridge but quickly realised she was too much of a day dreamer to be a serious scientist. She discovered that making telly is a great way to explore new topics, venture into other people's lives and try and explain them through storytelling.

She loved writing stories as a kid and in an effort to stop procrastinating and start writing fiction again she joined the North Bristol Writers Group. Despite making documentaries for a living she spends her spare time obsessively watching dramas and particularly crime series. These are the inspiration for her story in the anthology, her first detective mystery.

Justin Newland was born a stubborn Capricorn too long ago to remember.

He lives in Somerset with his girlfriend and writes historical, fantasy and speculative fiction with a supernatural bent. Excerpts of his work have entertained listeners at readings over the last few years at various events in the Bristol area. He was delighted to appear as a panellist at BristolCon 2013 and has published a short story in an anthology entitled *Hidden Bristol*. He has been a member of writers' groups in Bath and Bristol.

Currently, he is writing the first novel of his magnum opus, a pre-apocalyptic trilogy entitled *The Genes of Isis*. Find more information, go to his author web site www.justinnewland.com or the trilogy web site www.thegenesofisis.com.

Margaret Carruthers has lived in Filton, Bristol for 40 years with her husband. They share their home with a cat and a chicken. They have a son who has moved out of the family home. After retiring, she spends her free time reading all kinds of fiction from fantasy to crime. She joined NBWG last year and enjoys writing tales from fantasy, horror and crime. Her one novel is for sale on Kindle, and she is in the process of sending the novel into an online monthly magazine one chapter each issue.

Desiree Fischer is a writer who lives in Bristol with her partner. She is originally from a small town in south-west Germany, but she knew from approximately the age of five that she wanted to live in England. She enjoys the challenge of writing in a language that's not her mother tongue and while her writing focuses mostly on Science Fiction & Fantasy, she isn't averse to trying her hand at other genres. She is a new addition to the BristolCon Committee and is very passionate about promoting local authors as well as new voices like herself.

Roz Clarke is a recent addition to the North Bristol group, having previously been a member of the long-standing Monday Night Group in Manchester, and having spent the last few years pinging across the country between Bristol and That London. She's a graduate of the Manchester Metropolitan University Creative Writing MA and of Clarion West. She's had short stories published in various magazines and anthologies, most notably *Black Static* and *Dark Spires*. She is also co-editor of the anthologies *Colinthology* and *Airship Shape & Bristol Fashion*, alongside Joanne Hall. She's been a member of the BristolCon committee since its inception in 2009, and is delighted to have come to rest in this peculiar, inspiring city. Roz blogs at www.firefew.com.

Kevlin Henney writes shorts and flashes and drabbles of fiction and books and articles on software development. His fiction has appeared online and on tree (*Litro, New Scientist, Physics World, LabLit, The Pygmy Giant, The Fabulist, Word Gumbo, Kazka Press, Dr. Hurley's Snake-oil Cure* and others) and has been included in a number of anthologies (*The Salt Anthology of New Writing 2013, Eating My Words, Scraps, Jawbreakers, Flash Me! The Sinthology,*

Fifty Flashes of Fiction, The Kraken Rises! and *Kissing Frankenstein & Other Stories*).

As well as having his work rejected and making no impression whatsoever on writing competitions, Kevlin's stories have been longlisted, shortlisted and placed, and he won the CrimeFest 2014 Flashbang contest. He reads at spoken word events, winning the National Flash-Fiction Day Oxford flash slam in 2012, and has performed his work on local radio (BBC Radio Bristol and Ujima). Kevlin organises the Bristol Flash events for National Flash-Fiction Day.

He lives in Bristol and online. He can be read on his blog at http://asemantic.net/ and stalked on Twitter as @KevlinHenney.

C M Hutt is a mature student studying Drawing and Print at the University of the West of England. She is also a member of the BristolCon committee and organiser of their monthly Fringe readings. She co-edited a zine called *Full Frontal Lobe* where she published her first illustration, *Inner Workings of a Ray Gun*, and her short story *Verne's Rise*. She has also had an illustration in an anthology called *Felinity* for the short story *No Tears*. Her work can be found at www.cmhutt.com, on Facebook at C M Hutt Art or on Twitter @clairedreams99.